One Small Saga

BOBBIE LOUISE HAWKINS :: A NOVELLA

Introduction by Laird Hunt & Eleni Sikelianos

Interview with the author by Barbara Henning

Including the short story "En Route"

LOST LITERATURE SERIES #29
UGLY DUCKLING PRESSE :: BROOKLYN, NY :: 2020

One Small Saga and "En Route" are republished with the permission
of Sarah Creeley, and with the invaluable assistance of Sarah Elizabeth
Schantz. *One Small Saga* was originally published by Coffee House
Press in St. Paul, Minnesota in 1984, designed by Allan Kornblum, with
composition by Annie Graham. The design of this republication emulates
the original edition, though without the title calligraphy by Glenn Epstein.
The story "En Route" included in this edition did not appear in the book
One Small Saga—it was originally published as a chapbook in 1982 by
Little Dinosaur Press, Albany, California.

Lost Literature Series #29
ISBN 978-1-946433-64-0
First Edition, First Printing, 2020

Ugly Duckling Presse
The Old American Can Factory
232 Third Street #E-303
Brooklyn, NY 11215
www.uglyducklingpresse.org

Distributed in the USA by SPD/Small Press Distribution
Distributed in the UK by Inpress Books
Distributed in Canada by Coach House Books via Publishers Group Canada

Design and typesetting by Don't Look Now! and C. Bain
The type is Sabon

Books printed offset and bound at McNaughton & Gunn
Covers printed letterpress at Ugly Duckling Presse

The publication of this book was made possible, in part, by a grant
from the New York State Council on the Arts, a state agency.

NEW YORK STATE OF OPPORTUNITY. | Council on the Arts

Contents

Introduction

Like her good friend the writer Lucia Berlin, Bobbie
Louise Hawkins was an excellent observer of others. Like
Lucia, too, she was wise and damn funny. Her stories are
vitamin-packed, full of her own, specific and inimitable
possibilities of voice. Or maybe we should say voices, or
voicings, because the singular doesn't quite do it justice. In
person, her voice could take on multiple angles and colors,
depending on the setting and time of day, the interlocutor,
or, more accurately, the listener, and the number. It wasn't
unusual to hear her with a Texas drawl in the morning in
her garden (this voice said "Honey" a fair amount, and
unfurled like a smoked tumbleweed just rolling out of the
fire), a soft New Mexican clipping of word endings in the
afternoon, and a British tilt at a party in the evening. Her
voice could even take on several aspects at once, especially
when she was giving a reading. Voicing was important
enough to Bobbie that she offered classes on how to talk
(and *not* talk) into a mic. Don't pop those *p*s! Make sure
you cut the mic! No heavy breathing between words!

And while *One Small Saga* is not as voicey as some of her other work, her marvelous capacity to listen and deftly mimic is acutely on display. She speedily gets her world and her characters "in" as E.M. Forster, a writer whose prose she admired, put it. Consider one quick sentence early on, the short passage that takes place in Mr. Collins' sitting room. Bobbie builds this Englishman's whole character out of just a handful of syllables. The narrator has just noticed the wall hangings, "patterned blue and white cotton to match the drawn drapes. [...] 'Nigerian,' Mr. Collins told me, seeing me looking, 'handwoven native.'" In three tight-lipped words we get the tone of the whole of the British empire circa 1950, from the mouth of one of its servants.

Still, in this autobiographical work (Bobbie claimed not to have done any other kind), what's mainly going on is an attempt at taking the measure of the life the narrator wants to live. She starts that process by recounting a mistake that isn't a mistake at all. She does something stupid (marries Axel) to get to the next thing (the story of her life). How else would a ferociously observant , intelligent, original young woman born into poverty in the 1930s get out of the fix she is in? She has plans, inchoate as they are, and takes the ship that will get her started, pointed firmly in the direction of elsewhere. That the ship she travels on has a "green marble swimming pool" hidden in its depths, which she soon finds herself plunging into daily, seems emblematic. Like Bobbie, the narrator of *One Small Saga* has an unerring ability to sniff out the unlooked-for and the exceptional.

"You want to put yourself adjacent to the most interesting person in the room," Bobbie liked to say to her students (we were two of them). Bobbie herself, of course, was very often that most interesting person, but if she was never under-cognizant of this particular fact of the matter—and why should she have been?—that discerning eye of hers turned ever outward. You can see the narrator looking for compelling adjacencies all though *One Small Saga*. If at first she has to contend with bipedal oafs like Axel's insufferable sister—"I smiled at Birte. It was very like smiling at a locomotive."—the circle expands as the story takes us and the narrator through London, Jamaica, and elsewhere, and by its end a critical mass of interesting acquaintance has been achieved. Along the way, both the novella and its narrator have expanded their capacities to accommodate. The last sentences, in fact, deftly, brilliantly present us with several stories at once. There is the woman doing the remembering and the woman being remembered. Against these two, who are at once the same and different women, is thrown, in excruciating relief, the major's wife. She is not so much a character as an apparition: a woman who did not grok what her own next thing was or how to get there. She is stuck there in the past with her choices and her bandaged wrists.

The narrator, however, has made more than several lives for herself since that juncture. She doesn't need to go into them. We know it because she is elsewhere, in a state of remembering. The doubling and tripling of meaning, the deep care for both herself and for the major's wife that is encapsulated in that final sentence, "How could I have forgotten?" is nothing short of stunning.

By the short story "En Route," also included here, and which is an episode from her later marriage to the American poet Robert Creeley, Bobbie has *clearly* put herself adjacent to the most interesting persons in the room. However difficult that marriage also proved, she enormously relished the conversation and mind of it and spent a significant part of the years after its dissolution untangling its many stories.

Bobbie was, above all else, a storyteller, a potent one. One who could stick her landings and shape the hell out of her sentences: "The desires of the heart do rise up at the least jogging. The heart stands high and looks for miles at the least excuse." One who developed, as she turned to teaching, violent antibodies to infelicitous utterance. Once I (this is Laird) gave her a story to read that was full of short "i" sounds. Think "pin" "gin" and "sin." "Oh, good Lord, Honey," she said. She looked both anguished and angry as she smashed her pen through each offensive instance. Was it that there was too much complaint in all that "ih, ih, ih" sound? Not enough of the round, full vowels of creation?

To the ancient Greeks, being a storyteller meant you could weave the opening stuff of the world, which was chaos, into *muthos*, also known, Bobbie's friend Charles Olson reminds us, by the term myth. This is not any Christian sense of that term, but a self-making. If you don't believe in heaven and hell, Bobbie tells us, "then you don't get the simplified up and down. The pattern is instantly random and the options are more like something hit the floor and splattered." What you do with the splatter is up to you.

Some storytellers are also talkers, and Bobbie, as we hinted at above, was one of those. She often talked about gardens and flowers, because besides being a storyteller and a talker and a fierce editor she was a world-class gardener. Why have I (this is Eleni) jotted down, in an old note about Bobbie, "the hero of her own journey"? I guess because, like the narrator of *One Small Saga*, she was. For example, she wasn't afraid to rip everything out and start from scratch; there would be murdered daylilies strewn across the walk, much to everyone's shock, and no one believed she could make a better garden than she already had, but then she did. When we moved to Boulder to teach at Naropa, one of the first things she said to me is, "Cleomes. You're gonna want cleomes." I soon learned she was not wrong.

— Laird Hunt & Eleni Sikelianos, 2020

One Small Saga
(1984)

The Bride

In late November on a warm afternoon with no breeze in it a man and a woman sat high up a gravelly slope overlooking the thin thread of water still called the Rio Grande.

We had shed our sweaters into a small pile on either side, his and hers.

There's that intimacy in even the slightest stripping, Oh, do let me help you with your wraps, my dear, and why not forever while we're about it.

He had just proposed marriage again.

I was quiet but not as if I gave it serious consideration.

It would serve him right if I said yes.

What to consider as if the house were burning.

I looked sideways at this eligible suitor. Pale hair slightly curling. Pale eyes. An immediately intimate smile. An insistently cheerful disposition. Tenacity.

I wondered at it.

I seemed to myself such an unlikely candidate for so Jane Austen an advantage.

KING KONG had played in a movie house in Lagos in Nigeria for twelve years. For a few cents apiece, Axel said, Africans who came to town out of the bush had made it a weekly ritual.

The print of the film was old and scratched. The giant ape appeared from and disappeared into mists of light, a radiant fabric, a magic shining of scratched film.

The movie house, a warehouse room, would be filled with African blacks watching Hollywood blacks say "Magumba!" and "Kumbawa!"

They watched a Hollywood ape with mad glass eyes crash free, destroy the El, climb the Empire State Building.

When the time came for the ape to be shot down the room would be very quiet.

And he would fall.

In Denmark no one would think to marry a virgin.

(This was 1950.)

So that was that; no problem that only yesterday would have been an admission. Not really shameful, more usual than acknowledged. But now it seemed it was a bonus.

"Who wants all that mess," he asked.

"I don't," he answered.

He had been first a blond head poked around the screen put just inside the studio door to keep passersby from looking in at the nude models. (Window washers had a field day.) He was a blond head and an English accent asking whether there was an office for the Art Department and where it might be.

I was standing wiping paint off a fistful of brushes with newspaper.

I stopped, my hands filled, gave him directions.

He bobbed thanks and disappeared.

"There's no one here. Do you think they've gone for lunch?"

"They should be back by one-thirty."
He was in full figure and smiling.
I'd thrown the wads of newspaper into the bin and was swishing the bristles in turpentine.
What were colors had melted to mud on my hands.
"I haven't had lunch," he said. "Would you like to go to lunch?"

The brushes were washed, rinsed, wiped damp dry, put stems down in a mason jar where the cleaned heads fanned out in a damp bouquet.
It was already an age-old story.

He took me to lunch. Took me to dinner. Took me to lunch the next day and showed me chess moves.
And proposed marriage.
He didn't want to return to Denmark and remarry his first wife who was making overtures. He didn't tell me that.

He said I should leave this place. I agreed and would have been gone long ago but didn't know how.
Even with all he implied, I told him No.
I wanted over the falls in a mindless rush. Love is when you can't help yourself.
He said that could all come later.
"It would be different if there were more time," he said.

The Rio Grande has shrunk with age and demand. Its banks hold, spread wide in a fixed memory of better days.
Now it is mostly sand with stands of tamarisk and cottonwood along the edges.
The cottonwoods were filled with dried brown leaves, all their fiery gold faded.
He hadn't seen that. At least I knew more about this place where we were than he did.

He had no idea that his worldly knowledge, which he meant to be tempting, Europe and London and Africa, also caused me to look askance.

I was not so charmed as he was by the sense of myself as young and precocious and malleable. I was not so charmed that he saw me as improvable and himself as my transforming agent.

When I implied I liked myself well enough he would smile and know better.

It was all very unsatisfying for him.

This young woman did not know that in his own environment, in Lagos, where he was chief architect and manager of his English firm's West African branch, he was a more than usually desirable bachelor. Mothers invited him to dinner as a hope for their unmarried daughters.

He had never thought to marry an American.

His friends had said, "Don't come back with an American wife," and it had been a joke. It took no thought at all.

His sense of American women was of females with their hair frozen in place, dressed in pastel nylon. Voices located in nasal passages.

"You don't sound like an American," he said, and meant it to be a compliment.

He watched her look down the valley and not say Yes and he wondered whether it might simply be that she was ignorant of true values.

If she agreed to marry him and they left this place would she, once they were beyond those mountains, change? Would she know what mattered? And knowing it would she respond appropriately?

If not, what a burden it would be to have a wife who might, through youthful ignorance, go vague in the very face of worth.

"If you marry him would your children be American or
Danish?"
"Oh, I don't know. You can probably choose."
"Well, you'd make them be American, wouldn't you?"
My mother stood in the sunshine holding a willow pattern cup in her left hand, a square of unbleached muslin in her right.

He tempted me deliberately.
He said, "If you don't want to stay you can come back. We can always get a divorce. A divorce isn't so much."
He said, "If you'd rather, we can have a trial marriage for a year and see at the end of it whether we want to marry."
He even suggested to my mother that we could have a trial marriage.
He suggested the trial marriage to my mother as a way to reassure her. My mother was not reassured.
But I was impressed that he did it.
It amazed me that he did it.
I was impressed enough to say Yes on the strength of it.

In Florida they were teaching porpoises to talk.
The announcer said that in captivity the porpoises lower their voice pitch toward the range of their human captors.
"If that isn't the silliest thing!" my mother said.
"What would *you* do," the announcer asked, "if an intelligent life form had you caught in an air-filled case and you must try to communicate with them?"
"I think I'll go with Axel," I said into the room.
If someone had made a joke of it I might still have been stopped.
"Well, if that's the way you want it, honey."

And he?
He twisted slightly.
Had he been enjoying an increasing security in my refusals?

"Well?" I asked when we stepped outside into the night. My eyes felt altered by decision. Was it a decision?

"I wish you had said something to me first. It's all right to surprise your mother but you might have found a more private time to tell me."

I knew he was right but thought he really wanted us to act as if we were in love.

And why not.

In love or not it was a romance.

The desires of the heart do rise up at the least jogging. The heart stands high and looks for miles at the least excuse.

The engagement was effected.

We regarded one another, intent. The night sky darkened. We were in each other's life. The moon was a definite and vivid crescent. Very thin. Very thin. The ancient horns.

On the morning of the wedding day a snapshot was taken of the couple. They are standing in the backyard of a small square house. Some clothes have been washed and are hanging on a line to the right. The groom-to-be is wearing crepe-soled shoes and a belted jacket. The bride-to-be is wearing Levi pants and a man's white shirt. A bandanna is tied around her head to hide the curlers. She means to be beautiful later.

It was a grander solution, that marriage, than any I could have dreamed of prior to the arrival of Axel in his belted jacket. I was at the end of my rope and the rope itself had been an invention.

I had borrowed money from a loan company to pay the first half of a semester's tuition (Fine Arts Department, University of New Mexico, Albuquerque). My plan was to find a job that would both leave me free during the day so I could go to class and pay me enough money to let me repay the loan while I saved toward the second half of the tuition.

I found no job that fit the projection.

When Axel appeared in the doorway I was dead broke and stopped. I had no money for the loan's current payment and I had no money for the balance of the tuition. In painting class I had come to be more experimental daily as I used up tubes of color and made do with what was left. My drawing teacher thought I showed up at class after class with only a newsprint pad and charcoal because I couldn't be bothered to bring whatever he had assigned as that day's media. He told me that earlier he had thought of me as someone with promise, someone special, and I was a disappointment.

I knew that I could explain to him so he would know I was not shirking. And I knew that if I tried to explain I would begin crying. I was not insensitive.

I did not try to explain.

All my hopes for self-improvement had brought me to no next move, no resource for one more step.

And in my more intimate daily life I was not only not a virgin but I had been brainwashed to believe I would pay for that failing, and to feel (I can't call it thinking) that without a great deal of luck and perseverance (in what I don't remember) I could only go downhill.

At nineteen I was blighted and stopped.

And then...

I was married, all unknowing, by an FBI agent.

He was the minister for the St. John's African Holiness Church.

I was a member of the NAACP and so was he.

When I needed a preacher he was the only preacher I knew. People more sophisticated and knowledgeable than I was and am have been taken in by FBI agents in whatever drag their cover story required.

I learned the truth of it when I returned to Albuquerque six years later.

Of course I've always assumed he really *was* a preacher and we really *were* married.

• • •

It took just two weeks from the day they met for the handsome Dane to marry his young wife and put the two of them aboard a Greyhound Bus, en route to Africa.

They would stop to see his sister, Birte.

They would stop in New York City.

They would stop in Denmark.

They would stop in London.

Then they would take the last leg "home."

Birte told Axel of the cheap passage she had found to Denmark.

An old Swedish liner, the *Gripsholm*, reclaimed from the bone-yard to be a hospital ship during the war, was now a passenger ship for travelers with no grand expectations. Birte would be on it with her two children in ten days. After Christmas in Denmark she would go to her own house in London and be joined there by her excellent husband, Gilbert, in mid-January.

Gilbert, who never spoke when Birte was talking, stood at the piano picking out calypsos with one finger.

Axel telephoned.

In ten days Axel and I would also be aboard the *Gripsholm*.

Axel did not think of himself as capricious.

When he was younger he had, for a bet and a dare, stripped naked and jumped off the railing of a Swedish freighter in a pitch black night to fall far down into the unknown waters of a Russian harbor where they were moored. His instantly sobered companions had called a deckhand and

he had been got back aboard without much trouble.
He enjoyed heroic status for the rest of that voyage.

"You are *insane*, my dear Axel! You are quite *insane!*"
Birte laughed as she spoke. She cut her own hair and the
thick-cropped shelf showed her thick neck. She spoke vig-
orously and laughed. Her eyes were blue and critical, taking inventory. When she laughed she exposed large strong
teeth. When she walked the floor shook.
"You are such *romantics!*" she said to me, meaning nothing admirable.
Birte had survived the Battle of Britain. Birte had hated
the American soldiers who arrived in London saying
"Remember Pearl Harbor."
"They married the worst women imaginable. I must say we
cheered them on. It looked for a time as if the Americans
might be the solution to cleaning up Piccadilly. All the
whores went to America as war-brides." She smiled at me.

I said Yes and meant it.
I meant to be a wife however confused I might be by the terms.
In my heart of hearts I had made promises to the future. I
would do my best to not botch it.
I meant to do it right.
I meant all sorts of things Axel had no notion of.
I *would* get on with this beastly woman I was now related to.
I smiled at Birte.
It was very like smiling at a locomotive.

• • •

Hotel wallpaper.
Being caught in somebody else's idea.
Three thousand miles from what I knew best and farther
still to go.
Back is no direction.

Axel clicked suitcases, opened and closed drawers.
Axel began to whistle while he worked.
Axel meant to jolly me up.

In the meantime he suffered his own misgivings.
He was, after all, no Pygmalion.
Hard marble and a chisel to work it with are a far cry
from a lump of unmoving female and a cheerful whistle.
Still he whistled.
Hope can do no less.

I came out of bed glued to a tumble of covers. My feet
reached the carpeted floor and I stood, looked at the wall
for a count of ten, headed for the bathroom with the
lurching unevenness of an adolescent.
Axel sighed a sigh of exasperation and relief. And when
I came back out of the bathroom carrying the toothpaste
and my toothbrush I smiled. Not vibrantly. Not coura-
geously. But it was a smile.

New York City was ready for Christmas.
The taxi that took us to our ship drove past windows
filled with seasonal displays. In one an animated Jack
jumped over his candlestick and turned to jump again.
And Peter stood beside his pumpkin shell with its closed
door and its window open to show Mrs. Peter within in a
state of domestic felicity, her head nodding and nodding,
a constant smile on her face.

America, Birte told me at dinner, did not have Bach or Beethoven or Karl Marx. America did not have Paris, the Greeks, or the Renaissance. America did not have Europe. And Birte, it seemed, did.

Birte spoke four languages, had a superior education, was married to a superior person. She came from a superior family from a superior country which did not preclude her being a holder of democratic views.

And I was not to take the taxi-driver from Chicago who shared our third-class table as representative of the type of person I would be associating with once we arrived in Denmark.

I said little in return.

Being overwhelmed by Birte was an acceptable response.

I did not envy the First Class passengers their carved Victorian bars, lounging rooms with flowers on writing tables.

I envied them for not having Birte.

Axel found a green marble swimming pool in the depths of the ship.

He found it by asking to look at the ship's plans.

And there it was, with its own little elevator up to all the levels of all the decks.

He went to where he had seen the elevator on the plans, pushed the button, went down. He came out of the elevator into a room the size of a high school gymnasium, fitted out like one. A bit more exotic. There were electric horses that could be set at three gaits. There were belts to trim the figure by shaking the body. There were barbells and dumbbells. And through a door at the room's far end was a smaller room just large enough to hold a full-size swimming pool with six feet around it to be walked on.

The pool was filled with blue-green water. A switch on the wall turned on lights at the pool bottom and made a light-show of wavering lines on the walls. The pool was green marble with curved steps at one end. Green marble pillars were every five feet along the other three sides. Each pillar held a brass ring and through the ring a thick wine-red velvet rope was threaded, making scallops around the pool.

Axel got permission to use the pool on the basis that he tell none of the other passengers about it.

We took towels daily and made our way along the iced deck to the elevator door. We spent our afternoons in the pool and the adjacent sauna.

I stopped sleeping.

It's the old songs we love the best... anxiety and floating phrases... not all the time just chunks of it...

I stopped sleeping.

I like high-class myself they get all that extra room for the generous moves ... and Hi-Yo, Silver ... Heigh-Ho as in Tote that barge?

I stopped sleeping.

Pills from the ship's doctor had a reverse effect given the dinner and the booze and the pigs' heads with items of fruit lodged between the opened lips on the corners of the tables and paper elves holding hands and dancing in long cut-out strips the length of the tables while the after-dinner speeches dealt with variations on Scandinavian-Scandinavian Brotherhood and Scandinavian-American Brotherhood and the Norwegians and Danes went tight-lipped at the Swedes saying so, the war being too close and Hitler using Sweden as a footpath to get to everywhere else.

Next day the Swedes left. All the barriers that designated the classes of passengers were taken down. The ship opened to be one big party all the way to the other two countries.

Two Danish reporters who came aboard in Sweden found Axel's name on the passenger list and sought him out to ask him whether he was related to his father. Herr Politimester Raasloff commanded all the Danish police forces, an appointment from his friend, the King. When the Nazis had entered Denmark, Herr Raasloff had been one of the first persons to be put in a cell. Axel explained to me that his father's position was nothing like being a policeman in the United States. His father's position was more prestigious and more honorable though it seemed it did not pay well. The honor was the thing.

NEWLYWEDS ON HONEYMOON was the story the reporters got, and pictures of the couple with confetti and streamers caught to their hair and shoulders.

During the interview Birte bristled, irritated by the lack of attention she was getting in all this.
She reminded them all that Axel was, in fact, her father's stepson while she is truly her father's daughter. One of the reporters mollified her with questions. She was satisfied until two days later when she saw the newspaper, with its headline and its large picture of her brother and his wife, and found that only the slightest mention had been made of her own presence.

• • •

This day of the small rain, the gray sky: this day was ours.
This landing place, flags flying, confetti caught to our hair, tendrils of streamers caught to our coats.
On the dock a red-coated band was playing shining brass.
The dock below was filled with upturned faces.
The *Gripsholm* had risen into the sky and these were our own dear heliotropes.

Axel and Birte scanned the crowd for familiar faces.

"There they are! They're waving!"

Birte snatched her daughter Squiggles high to wave to Grand-Mama and Grand-Papa.

Squiggles had been told of the rail and doom, and shrieked at being swung so easily into jeopardy.

She was put down and clung sobbing to the skirts of her own Mommy-monster.

Birte's son, Charles, stood stalwartly watching, apparently unmoved, very English, very masculine, very much the nine-year-old young man who could take it all in stride.

We came to earth in the drafty, echoing Customs building.

Change the country. Change the name.

"*Girl of my dreams*" ... Set to start again and do it better this time.

I held onto Axel's arm. I smiled wanly, pale and not at my best.

I am a crumpled version and defenseless.

We all stood under a giant "R," though soon Birte would go to stand under "M."

"My father could have exempted all our bags from inspection but he would never do such a thing," she told me, and smiled in triumph at being like everyone else but by a moral choice.

She also told me, "This will be a very good Christmas for you. We do not use electric lights on the tree."

"*When my dream boat comes home,*" sang in my head, Birte won't be on it.

We went to the home of an Aunt who lived in Copenhagen. Tante Anna had married a Frenchman. He had lived in Denmark now for thirty years and still spoke only French. His wife cheerfully translated for him even though

it was clear he understood all that was said. After dinner
I slipped away to a front room to look at Copenhagen
through the parlor window's lace curtains. They found me
there, sleeping, sitting in a small chair with my elbows on
the window sill, my chin resting in my hands.

Fru Raasloff led me through the house to a small cold
bedroom and tucked me under a goosedown cover.

Axel stood in the doorway explaining at length to his sister Gena, who was as thin as Birte was fat.

"Well," she said to him, her voice sour, "you've got yourself a child-of-nature."

Jørn the beautiful boy, eight years old, his yellow hair and eyebrows a line straight across his face, red-cheeked and vigorous, tramps the coastline in all weather. He stands, eyes blue as birds flown to the horizon to return in their own good time. His boots are made of heavy black rubber and mash their print into the sand in his wake. He returns in the late winter afternoon back along his tracks to his own garden's gate. Over his head bare branches twine and mesh in a lacework canopy. The last of the pearly twilight seeps coldly through, and the garden, darkening at the corners, grows larger. The sitting room window flickers with warm color through the crooked fruit trees. A scraggy skeleton of lilac scratches his coat as he passes to go through the kitchen door.

The kitchen air is steamy and flavored. Armandine, her face shiny, moves among the clutter of cutlery, crockery, rag-ends of trimmed fat. She smiles at him and wishes him good evening. A light sweat of steam covers the boy's face as he supports himself, hand on the wet wall, and fights his boots off. In the narrow pantry window at his side all the panes of glass have run stripes of small rivers from the top to the bottom.

The house is in threefold celebration: Christmas is near; the family is together; Axel has brought home a bride. They are all in the sitting room. Their faces are lighted by candles among pine boughs on the room's central table. It is the fire that lights the walls around them and shows the old-fashioned room more clearly with its pictures and heavy, comfortable furnishings. They turn to welcome him in, their most recent seafarer. He circles the room formally, shaking hands with each of them and bobbing his head.

Fru Raasloff is the room's coquette: charming, demanding, her gestures youthful. Her daughters are her tragedy. Birte

sits in a chair, large and heavy, with a jolly maliciousness. Gena, thin and quince-mouthed, soon to be divorced, sits on the curving loveseat. They are the traditional "two ugly sisters." They have never learned to "enter" a room. "Ah," Fru Raasloff will say in the next breath after such a sad admission, "but my *sons* are delightful!"
Axel and Jørn were accustomed to their mother's unqualified approval.

Fru Raasloff is attempting English for her new daughter-in-law.
She names something, adds a verb. It makes no sense. Her hands define graceful shapes in the air. There is the feel, the broken rhythm of a motor that won't catch. At last, making a face of mock despair, she speaks a whir of Danish, ends with a peremptory circle of her right hand. "Tell her," she says in English, and relaxes back, smiling and nodding, while Birte, smiling, translates for the bride.

I am attentive. I care very much that I should be liked. I smile at anyone who looks at me. The smallest politeness enlarges in my grateful consideration. I say Thank you when I mean to say Good evening.
Birte's exposition translates a graceful Danish to an abrupt English.
"She says how could your mother have let you go so far away with a man you only knew for two weeks?"

It could have been said many ways. Fru Raasloff has perhaps said it differently. This is the way Birte will always say it.
Muddled by my new sister-in-law's meanness, I answer that my mother trusted my judgment.
"He looks to be trustworthy," Axel's father says in English. They all look at Axel. Pale blue eyes. Cheerful smile. They all believe that a mother might trust him.
"Love will find a way," Axel's father adds.

Fru Raasloff smiles fondly at her son and at his young wife.
The moment is past.

It seems that I am a novelty. So young a bride to not be
pregnant.
In Denmark, they tell me, no one marries younger than
twenty-five without special permission from the King.
He always grants permission when asked.
Everyone knows what the king's permission means.
Sour-faced Gena's marriage and first child came under
Royal auspices.
Eight years of marriage and a second child have not re-
deemed Gena's professor/husband in the eyes of her family.
"So foolish! to get a girl pregnant!"
And now they are proven right.

Gena's domestic collapse has provided us with a house of
our own, a honeymoon cottage.
We bicycle the two miles between the houses.
We eat and bathe and visit with the family in the family
home.
We sleep and wake and have some privacy in the limbo
of this house that will be disposed of according to the
divorce decree.
Yellow-stuccoed, two stories high, it sits off on its own
road, as bleak in this Danish winter as the regulated hatred it has held.
There have been no passionate arguments in these rooms.
They reek of dry-eyed endurance.

Only the study, exorcised by walls of books, can be sat in.
I sit, hugging my chest, overheating the round-bellied
stove with blocks of pressed peat, watching the cast-iron
fire to a glow.
On the other side of the wall, unseen, the paint blisters
away, flaking off the wall in protest.

"Jørn says that you let him come into the bathroom when
you were naked in the tub."
It is Gena who speaks.

The smell is food and waxed furniture.
We are all at lunch.
The dining table is covered by a heavy linen cloth.
Between the table and the kitchen Armandine moves in a
clean white apron.
Armandine's apron is starched so stiff that it will crack
like thin white stone and shatter but it will never wrinkle.

Foolish!
Foolish and mistaken.
Axel has told me that they all swim naked in the summer
and I have taken that for an ease with nakedness. Now it
seems in this instant of all their faces turned toward me
that the ocean allows nakedness and the bathtub is taboo.

"He knocked to say he had left something. I said he could
get it."
Gena is smiling a tight lipped smile. Another pin put in.
"She thinks I'm a fool," I think.

I have never darned a sock.
"What do you do when socks have holes in them?"
"We throw them away."
Now they must question the wife Axel has brought home,
an American wife after all, who has never darned a sock.
"They are cheap. We buy new ones."
"She means cotton," Axel says, "and nylon. It is warmer
there."

After dinner Fru Raasloff brings out her basket of wools,

places it between us and begins to teach me. I'm reassured and cozy in the rightness of it.

I mean to have a different life.

I also feel it is a proper bride's occupation, learning to darn socks.

The family eases back.

There is a party where the bride wears a bride's dress, white and sheer chiffon with long sleeves falling in soft folds to a narrow band at the wrists. Draping folds over the breast catch to a wider band at the waist. A full skirt falls in soft pleats to the floor.

She wears a small pin of blood-red garnets, a gift from Fru Raasloff.

"I have worn it many years," Fru Raasloff tells her. And as if they have a secret, "My daughters... it would not suit them. It will suit you exactly."

The bride wears the pin on a thin velvet ribbon around her neck.

The two ugly sisters, when she is near, cannot keep their hateful eyes off the red garnets on the black ribbon on the white skin.

Axel wears a dark blue suit, a white shirt, a red bow-tie, a satisfied expression.

He raises his glass to toast his young wife across the table.

Before-dinner drinks, beer and schnapps on the table, wine, champagne, brandy, liqueurs: it is a traditional and acceptable drunken celebration with speeches and toasts. One fattish man serves as the classic obscene guest. He no sooner sits than he lurches again to his feet to make another toast in Danish. The table roars. He is taken for wonderful. The groom's first wife is there with her fiancé and takes the look of a martyr when her husband-to-be reaches over and grabs at her breast. He is glaring at Axel. Fru Raasloff speaks down the table to a young man, the son of her first husband by his second wife: "On your father's deathbed," she tells him, "he said that I was the only woman he ever really loved."

The fat guest rises with his latest toast.

Fru Raasloff rises also.

At her back her chair tilts and crashes to the floor.

Carrying her wineglass, carried by her emotion, Fru Raasloff comes around the table, walks the length of the table smiling and in a dream. The bride rises, to be caught in a tearful embrace.

"Welcome to our family!" Fru Raasloff cries out in English.

Her champagne pours down the younger woman's back.

For dessert there are thin pastry cornucopias filled and spilling sweet red berries. There is cream whipped as thick as butter in a large crystal bowl and, to lift it out, a heavily patterned silver spoon.

London

The night-boat from Denmark to England gleamed: polished brass and waxed wood; dark red carpeting underfoot; excellent food.

"How well you speak the language," Axel was told by an Englishman.

"I'm Danish," he replied, glowing; a compounded compliment.

From the night-boat to the boat-train and Liverpool Street Station.

Slimed cement, mucky with train-station dirt; thin slop squished in bubbles around Axel's sponge-rubber soles. We walked along the train to reach the front and be off the tracks.

Overhead, a high sloped roof, grimed-over windows let through a filtered gray light in angled widening bars, to the interior far below.

War sucks color out.

Gray faces. Gray hats. Gray mouths. Eyes gone grim.

War and rationing. A deep harsh winter. Outside the sky was gray, darkened by the drizzling slant of rain. The faces we passed were a fish-white pallor in the air's thin water.

It would be lovely to have style superior to every occasion. We had no such hope. Oddments of luggage and over-stuffed paper bags. Three dozen eggs from Denmark and a huge chunk of cheese. We moved down the platform and through the station and into the street like a history of im-migrants. I hung back against a wall, my fingers cramped and fixed through strings that held parcels of paper that couldn't be put on the wet sidewalk.

Axel was one more pale stranger moving back and forth along the curbing, ghostly, his right arm raised in a danc-er's curve over his head. The isolated and predictable dance of a man who hails a cab in the rain.

War is a monstrous mouth.
London had great bites eaten away, whole city blocks gone in a bite. The rubble was cleared away. Wallpaper and fireplaces floated up the sides of buildings that still stood.
Doors opened into the third floor, the fifth floor, as many floors as there were. No more fires. No more rooms on this side to be entered into. All those stories of happy-home got stopped.

Axel's act of passion had cost him Africa, temporarily. His courtship and honeymoon had caused him to so overstay his six-months' leave that someone else had been sent in his place. Now he had to stay and work in London for at least a year, possibly two.

Mr. Collins invited us to dinner.
Mr. Collins was long-boned and gawky. His lack of grace

seemed to be some kind of English value. It also seemed
to be a value that he spoke as if he had strings pulling out
on the corners of his mouth, flattening his words. It was a
Mayfair accent, Axel told me.

Mr. Collins parted his hair in the middle so it stood over
his forehead in a wiry kink of wings, a V that pointed
down to a large nose and a horsey jaw.

Mr. Collins's sitting room was cozy with drawn drapes
and lamps sitting in warm circles of light. A small fire
glowed red in the fireplace. On the mantelpiece were the
curves of three elephant tusks. They were carved into
three safaris of ivory elephants in single file.

The walls had hangings of patterned blue and white cotton to match the drawn drapes.

"Nigerian," Mr. Collins told me, seeing me looking,
"handwoven native."

Ostrich eggs held by red and blue strips of leather cut into
patterns hung in a cluster next to the fireplace.

Between the fireplace and the couch where I sat with Mr.
Collins was a small table that held my after-dinner coffee
and a tiny brass figure of a man balanced on a round platform the size of a silver dollar. Long brass wires curved
out and down from his shoulders to hold the weights that
balanced him and caused him to stand on the single pin-
point of his feet.

"Toy," Mr. Collins told me and reached to touch one of
the wires.

The small man careened and spun in a circle.

The base of the table that held the toy and the coffee had
once been an elephant's foot and a piece of its leg. The
toenails gleamed and the wrinkled skin was tanned leather. That table had died, been tanned and cleaned, been
stuffed and had its toenails polished.

"How did Axel persuade you to come away so quickly?" one of the adjacent ladies asked me.

"I decided to come when he told my mother that he understood that she must feel upset at the two of us not knowing each other and asked whether it would reassure her for the two of us to have a trial marriage for a year and then make up our minds."

"Extraordinary," the lady drawled. "And what did your mother say?"

"She said that wouldn't exactly reassure her."

"Charming," the lady laughed. The lady looked me over.

All the guests were old Africa hands and spoke knowingly. Number-one boy. Government House. Up-country. Exotic phrases rose and sank with the regularity of crocodiles in a Tarzan movie.

I reached for my coffee, lifted my cup from the table that had taken its last walk.

Spring would return. We both believed it.

To live by the Heath and walk out onto rough grass when the weather allowed would be nice, we thought.

With memories and a belief in Springs to come and the cold wind blowing fog through our bones we went to meander the hilly streets of Hampstead on the lookout for uncurtained windows that held no cats, no birds, no potted plants.

Buildings smashed flat by war had left too many people to fill what was left standing. We walked block after block and found nothing.

A grocer's window acted as a bulletin board and there was a filing card there that advertised "Garden Flat With Kitchen."

I thought of tulips as we walked along the street reading the numbers and arrived at an old brownstone with a cat, languid and elegant, looking out of the downstairs window.

The front door was a monstrosity of colored glass made into a pattern of triangles and diamonds and swung open instantly when we rang the bell as if the woman who opened it had been watching us come along the street.

She was fat with small piggy eyes and rice powder wiped over her face as if snow had fallen. She wore a linty hairnet made of hair over round curls pinned in place days earlier. Her plum velvet dress had a settled pattern of wrinkles with the nap worn away at the upper curve of the ridges. The V-neck was edged with scraggy fur and she wore dirty wine houseslippers with scraggy fur pompoms. Three cats of much the same sort of fur wound around her feet and looked up at us with no curiosity.

No, the flat had not been taken and she would be pleased to show it to us.

"It's a perfect place for a painter," she said as she led us along a narrow, dark hall which she referred to as ours. "This is your hall here. Then you go down these steps. And this is your door," which she opened onto a large basement room, low-ceilinged and square-shaped. One whole wall was covered by a large furnace and a maze of piping that disappeared up into the ceiling. The wall opposite held blue shelving with upright blue and white plates as décor.

The "kitchen" was a walk-in closet with no windows, lighted by a bulb that hung down on a ratty electric wire. A hotplate was on a shelf. The washing-up could be done in the bathroom, or water could be brought from the bathroom in an enamel pan.

The "garden" was a sooty bit of cemented yard where all the dustbins for the house were kept.

"Is this the furnace for the house?" Axel asked.

It was, and a man must come in to stoke it unless we'd like to stoke it ourselves for a lower rent.

A grand piano filled one corner of the room and must be left there.

The landlady had no idea of how it had been got in and no notion of how to get it out.

"It was here when I bought the place and it'll be here when I sell it. If I sell it."

We already knew it was not possible, this perfect happy nightmare of "the artist's life," with the stoker in and out and the untuned piano, but we went through with the rest of the tour.

We would share the bathroom with the lady who was our guide, her slippers flip-flopping and ourselves following after. "Your bathroom," she called it, and the three of us stood solemnly looking at the porcelain fixtures while she

explained that the curtains around the cast-iron tub were
for the privacy of the tenants, who were expected to leave
the door unlocked when they bathed as this was the only
way into a part of the landlady's "suite." She delicately
implied that we might lock the doors when we must use
the "other convenience."

"Of course, when I know someone's bathing I don't go
through unless I really must."

It was impossible, looking back into her little eyes fringed
with rice powder, to know quite what that might mean.

We saw other, less artistic rooms in other parts of London
and settled for a bed-sitting room in West Hampstead
with two single-bed couches, a small sink with cold water, a sixpence-metered gas heater with a burner attached
for cooking so near the floor that I sat cross legged on the
worn rug holding the off-center frying pan, if its contents
were lightweight, to keep it from dumping onto the floor.
We shared a "water-closet" and a bath where, in privacy,
one might drop a shilling into the geyser and have it ex-
plode in an open flame for a set number of minutes while
the tub filled.

A young couple owned the house. The wife was very pregnant and her mother protected her daughter's interests,
prowling the halls endlessly, suspicious and hardfaced.

Against this English winter my Danish father-in-law had given me two pair of long underwear, laughing when I insisted I could use them. One more charming Americanism. And it was true I needed them, having almost no warm clothing.

I wore my long underwear daily to the Slade where I still meant to learn to be a painter.

Over the long underwear I wore woolen stockings, denim Levi's, an itchy dark-blue wool sweater got from Army/ Navy Surplus where I had also got the smallest size of parachute trooper's boots.

Over all I wore an old sheepskin coat of Axel's.

It was warm and practical and markedly strange for London in 1950.

I stopped in Harrod's to buy a lipstick and a middle-aged Englishwoman passed me in the aisle, walked on another five feet and stopped, turned, looked at me with all the drama of a stage whisper from my neck down to the boots and back up again to the neck; turned to walk another three feet, turned back and did it all again.

And at a bakery near Knightsbridge Station a woman was leaving at the same instant I was arriving. Instead of the usual mutual move to the left and to the right the woman froze dead-center and said coldly, "Will you please move out of my way."

And I moved out of her way.

Hampstead Heath had hills, uncut wild grasses, stands
of trees, a brook, a real sky. It was very like being in the
country. People flew kites there on a high hill, children
with small paper-covered homemade jobs and a roughly
wound ball of string claimed equal rights with kites of
progressive splendor up to the grown man who flew a
giant contraption from a harness fitted around his body.
On windy days he would be jerked around and leaned
the whole weight of his body against the tug of a small
cable which came from the pit of his stomach to disappear in a slow curve into the sky. His kite when sight-
ed would be far to the left or right of where the cable
disappeared.

Axel and I came up out of the ground at Hampstead
Heath Station, turned right to walk up the hill, then left,
looking to locate the house number Hans had given me.
This occasion was a picnic to meet Hans's new wife. "She
is like a Rubens!"
In the basket Axel carried were deviled eggs, potato salad,
and a loaf of hard crusted bread with a sharp knife.

The hallway was dark as was the bed-sitting room. But
the kitchen was white and yellow with potted plants on
the wide sill of a large window. The day's lucky sunlight,
perfect for a picnic, poured through the plants and was
faintly tinged by them with a green that reflected on the
white walls.

The flat belonged to Hans. (Where did he paint, I wondered.) And now was clearly the place where he kept his
lady. Her garments were in little piles here and there, the
bed unmade. Some things were shoved under the bed and
the couch.
Passion?

It was true Alice was well-rounded, though small. Blond hair, very blue eyes, the look of her was emphasized by standing alongside Hans.

She ignored me after the introductions had been made and began to talk to Axel about how she wanted to travel.
"Life is so dull," she said.
"One must make amusements for oneself," she said in an affected, vivacious voice.
"I mean to travel. I'm not going to spend my life..." her voice faded. "I need clothes!" she interrupted herself to say to Hans, who sat quiet and miserable.
"I used to go to parties," and she began to name large hotels.
She would put on her party clothes, go to a hotel and take the elevator to the top floor. Then she would walk the length of the hall looking for a party. If there was no party on that floor she would go down to the next.
"There's always a party somewhere."
She knew where the most expensive suites in the hotels were and she'd try there first.
"They never know who all the women are. They might know the men but they never know all the women."
"Didn't anyone ever know you hadn't been asked," I asked.
"Oh, a few times. I said I was meeting my boyfriend there and I'd forgotten the room number but I was sure this was the floor."

Alice moved her chair closer to Axel and smiled at him. "I want to go to Paris. And Italy. And," archly as if now he could invite her, "I think I'd like Scandinavia. What's Denmark like?"
She turned her head, looking through Hans as if he weren't there.
"I love men with blond hair. I love blue eyes."

I thought we must have interrupted a quarrel that was continuing in this oblique fashion.
"We should get outdoors," I said to the other three.
"We can talk outdoors," I insisted.

Axel went to the bathroom.
Hans and Alice and I sat around the small table under the window waiting for him to return. Alice stopped talking when Axel wasn't there. I tried to make conversation but Hans was sunk in sadness and Alice wouldn't look at me so I stopped.
I watched the sun in the leaves, the sun we weren't out in. It was as rare and precious as gold.
I dreamed into the light and the leaves it shone through. As if my name had been spoken I came to myself in the awkwardness of how long Axel had been gone.
I looked at Alice but Alice was staring hatefully at Hans. I looked at Hans to find he had been watching me. His face was melting and tender and I blushed. The heat rose into my face.
Now Alice was looking at me, glaring with resentment.

Axel's return changed Alice's face utterly and she was a charming good-time girl again, all for him.
The small apartment and Hans were nothing compared to the good times she had known and would know again and the charms of this stranger.

We left carrying two hampers, the heath a short walk downhill past neighborhood shops, greengrocer, baker, fishmonger, art supplies.

We crossed the street at the corner and walked into the hills of grass. We passed the pond where children were sailing boats, setting the sails on the windward side of the pond and running a half circle to stand waiting while the

small craft would make its way across, curving and dip-
ping in every breeze. Or would founder in the center, sails
wrong, until someone would take a long stick and poke
the small boat toward a waiting hand.

It was a warm day. A light breeze blew warm.

For a time we walked alongside a rough gully hearing
the soft spring sound of water running along the bottom,
through a tangle of fresh greening brush.
We came to a straggling stop in tall grass on a hillside.
We trampled around to make a nest and sat in our clearing surrounded by the grass left standing.
Nothing was simple.

Alice chattered compulsively leaving something unsaid.
There continued to be the feeling, a stain on the time, that
something was being left unsaid despite Alice's obvious
intention to tell Axel everything.
He looked, she said, exactly like her first lover, also blond,
also blue-eyed. Hans, it was increasingly clear, looked
very different.

"The potato salad and the eggs are the way my mother
made them," Hans said to me.
Alice talked faster. She began to talk about the Slade,
where Hans and I were students. She implied that we
"met" there. Which we did. And went for coffee together.
And laughed together when the model, who was a week
into a month-long pose, went for a weekend to Brighton
and came in Monday morning a fiery red, her bikini strip-
ings laid onto her torso forever insofar as this pose was
concerned. And in one fell swoop all the carefully prepared palettes counted for naught.
But we did not "meet" there.
Still I was confused.

Did Hans think we "met" there?

No, I could not have so misunderstood him.
When he told me of his new wife he was happy.
Had he simply been hysterical?

The afternoon ended.
The time came for Axel and me to return to the station.
Alice and Hans walked us there.
Alice, walking ahead with Axel, still talked, describing herself as passionate, sensual, as having the attributes of women who only enjoy making love if the men are blond with blue eyes.
Hans and I, the dark ones, walked behind, quiet.

At the station Alice insisted that Axel should buy three tickets.
She meant to come along with us.
"I love you," she said, reaching for Axel's hand.
"I want to go with you."

We stood on the darkening platform missing our train again and again while Alice played the beleaguered heroine to whatever transient audience passed by. Hans reasoned with her, begged, humored, nothing would serve.
At last Hans held Alice forcibly while she screamed, "Don't touch me!" And at last we boarded a train.
Hissings and crashing metal.
Lights came on on the platform just before the train moved past the drama of Hans struggling with his Rubensesque wife, her arms flailing, mouth twisting.
And in the face, eyes clear and cold as decision. She had decided not to stay.

As the train entered the dark tunnel I no longer saw Hans and Alice but saw the vivid reflection of myself and Axel against the dark glass.

I looked at Axel's reflected face.

Bits of what passed in the world outside shot past and along his face with no impact. He rested back from his ordeal with his eyes closed.

"It would have been wiser not to kiss her," I said to the reflection.

"Of course it would have been wiser after the fact! How was I to know she was a raving maniac? I just took her to be a girl who wanted to be kissed back of a bush and I did it!"

I said no more.

He seemed so right.

But there was something wrong in it, even so.

I wanted nothing more than I wanted to be in the bath-
room vomiting.
My mouth was covered with my hand to hold it in.
I gulped at Birte, who had telephoned.
"Birte... I've got to go..."
"We'll be eating at seven-thirty but you should plan to arrive an hour before that."
"Birte... Axel will call you. I have to go now. I have to vomit."

"And two weeks ago when there weren't enough chairs Birte feels that you could have made a point of standing."
"What else?"
"She says you didn't thank her for the invitation."

•   •   •

My parachute trooper's boots were as good as any to start the waddling way toward motherhood.

"Will you be having a doctor or a midwife?"
"A *midwife*? I can choose a doctor or a *midwife*?"
(Visions of a New Mexican neighbor who assisted "at home," taking a three-pound package of new lard when she went. "She takes handfuls of it and crams it up when the baby's coming to help it slide out." "She opens a Bible and puts it under the pillow to keep the mother and the baby safe." "She opens a pair of scissors and puts them under the bed to cut the pain.")
The clinic nurse was Irish, a soft lilt to her questions.
"Do you mean to have the baby at home or in a hospital?"
"In a hospital. I want to have the baby in a hospital."
Looking down at the form on her desk, pen poised, the nurse asked, "First pregnancy?"
"Yes."
"Wait in there please. They'll call you."

She looked up, smiling, tipped her head to show where I must wait.

I was given an extra half-ration book and the right to buy a quart of milk a day for tuppence ha'penny. I went regularly to the clinic for powdered orange juice and vitamins and to have my pelvis measured with calipers. I liked having the extra bit of bacon, the extra bit of cheese, the extra bit of meat, the one more egg a week. My half-ration book announced my pregnancy in all the shops I regularly used. I could also buy bananas, when there were any, along with old people over sixty and children under twelve.

In August, when I was six months pregnant, we went for a weekend at Brighton. We stayed at a bed-and-breakfast. Breakfast was a badly cooked egg, half a tomato semi-cooked under a broiler, and two pieces of fried bread. I wore my old bathing suit on the beach. It fitted except for the extra bulge in my breasts and a smallish potbelly.

The next month I blossomed into an enormous round of myself and someone else lodged on the shelf of hip bones. We were not going to Africa at all.

We were going to the Caribbean for someone entirely different.

•   •   •

The colony was to be improved by the addition of a tourist hotel.

The hotel would not be palatial but its modesty was to be compensated for by services. An abundance of cheap labor is the traditional natural resource and commodity of under-developed countries. Servants would light cigarettes, shine shoes, care for small children, hand-launder clothing, carry breakfast trays to bedrooms and private verandas.

It was thought that the hotel might begin to attract a small share of the Caribbean tourist boom to the colony, now a poor and pathetic place with only lobsters for an export.

The plans for the hotel were made and drawn up in London in a government office by a civil servant who had never been out of England. The necessary data was available on paper. The guidelines were printed in a small booklet. The quondam architect used a map and a note on prevailing winds and the job was soon done.

The plans were copied in as many blueprints as would be needed; groundwork for limitless misunderstanding in time and space.
The mistakes, often grotesque, would occur at the other end and return to London as more paperwork to be solved on paper.

Various departments of the Colonial Development Corporation were activated by the plans. Bar stools and concrete and steel beams were ordered to be shipped. A wide range of skilled and semi-skilled labor was hired. A hotel manager was hired prematurely and would arrive to find himself with two years of salary and no hotel to manage.

Like a single handful of rice thrown onto the city from high overhead, the powers activated a small scatter of making ready.
Passports were renewed. The clothing allowances granted according to rank were spent. Passages were booked.

One Tuesday as a part of this sanctioned activity an order was being placed with a Bond Street tailor for two blue suits to be made up in tropic-weight wool.
The person bending his arms and legs to be measured was

Axel Raasloff recently hired by the Colonial Development Corporation to be the resident architect during the hotel's building.

The tailor, thin-faced and expressionless, elegant, would murmur in Axel's ear and Axel would hold a limb at an awkward angle while a yellow tape was spanned between one crucial point and another.

I sat, twenty and very pregnant, in a soft chair, a small table with an emptied teacup and saucer at my side, and watched the suits be invented into the air around Axel's slim figure.

The style of the occasion was impressive. A Bond Street tailor is no mean thing to see. A gesture of his hand created the fall the coat would have. A pinching turn of the thumb and forefinger showed where the trousers would hold a pleat.

Axel rose to the occasion. He demonstrated a settled taste in the cut a lapel should have and chose the dark blue he had hoped to find.

I watched in a daze of well-being. The soft chair, the tea, the murmur of voices beguiled my senses. I loved the slight smell of new cloth. I bathed in the atmosphere of new cloth. I could believe it now that we would leave London with its consistently unseasonable weather. We would go by ship to warm water and sunshine. Island beaches and palm trees unfolded forward in time from the London tailor's shop in an infinity of picture postcards. From this moment we were enroute to the tropics and to the house being prepared for us there.

I would be slim again in that place and wear cotton dresses with my arms bare and brown and dance with Axel in

one of his new suits at the Club he had told me would be
there.
We would swim in warm salty water. Calypso music and
moonlight.

At last the tailor brushed his client over with a soft bristle
brush as if to dispel the touching. A few platitudes floated
in the air to conclude the ritual.

Dazed with care and special attention, we went down
a flight of stairs and were reclaimed by reality. A quick
sharp wind chilled any inch of flesh that wasn't covered.
Axel tightened his wool scarf and I buttoned the small
very top button on my coat. The day was predictably gray,
the sun long since covered over with no hope of return.

At a Lyons Corner House we turned in through the door.
The warm air made our faces feel stiff. Our ears and cheeks
had turned red in the short distance we had walked. Axel
pulled the clean handkerchief he always carried from his
pocket to wipe his eyes and nose. "Just the blue I wanted."

We surveyed the cart of fancy pastries as if we surveyed
our altered prospects, slightly larger than life-size.
We celebrated the imagination of our future with fancy
pastry and a shared pot of steaming tea.

Jamaica

In dreams I'm in a small room and the ship is sinking.
I'm running for the door as the floor beyond it rises like
a water level.
The opening is disappearing as I'm running toward it. I
must climb to reach it, clinging to the upper door jamb
with the tips of my fingers.
All the while people are screaming where I can't see them.

• • •

We went up the gangplank. The gangplank was steady. It
was another winter departure.
Our cabin was larger, more comfortable. Our luggage was
already there.
Tea and drinks were in the upper lounge. Lunch would
wait for the sailing.

Axel wrote our names in for the second sitting in the dining room. It's how one avoids the children.

Another cold deck, slippery with rain and it was England we were leaving now.
Pigeons. Sparrows. Black-headed gulls. Swans on the Thames.
Ravens at the Tower of London. Massed flights of starlings. Hampstead Heath. Kew at lilac time. Hans with his shrieking wife.
Chiffon gowns in the windows at Harrod's.
Goodbye.
Goodbye.

Children racketed but the adults were mostly silent.
And the island was left.
No one stayed to watch it to the last. They'd all gone to lunch.
To the dining room rich with flowers and stiff shining linen.
To butter. Sugar. Menus with a choice.
I was embarrassed to feel such a rush of emotion at the sight of so much food.
"One good meal and I can't believe in suffering."

The first three mornings I ate a double breakfast. Orange juice and buttered toast and scrambled eggs, and sausages, and good coffee and sweet jams and marmalade.
Axel raised his eyebrows.
"Have you begun to eat for triplets, my dear?"
It was true I was burgeoning.
In that sudden dump outward women sometimes achieve in the last month of pregnancy my body had become unwieldy as if I carried a permanent piece of furniture. Overstuffed. It rocked me back on my heels, turned my toes out in a waddle, and curved my backbone.

When the stewardess caught sight of me her eyes widened
and she came to ask me specific questions.
Someone had made a mistake. A woman three weeks
away from delivery should never have been allowed onto
the ocean! Not on a ship *she* had any say over.
It was clear that I had been saved by my tent of a coat.
If the stewardess had a choice in it I would be put in one
of the rowboats, pointed toward England and left to my
own resources.

I saw the stewardess and the ship's doctor in grim conversation looking at me. A part of the conversation must be
the extent to which I was not following the stewardess's
advice to spend as much time as possible in bed.
"I feel fine!" I insisted, and saw her not be pleased. To the
stewardess it was as she had feared. If there was to be any
sensible worrying done it must all be done by herself. The
price one pays for authority.

Warmer waters and sunshine egged me on.
I was given the use of a bathing suit by a friendly fat
woman. It was a wrap-around of cotton. I tied myself into
it daily and went to the pool. Some of the more tradition-
al-minded adults on board made it clear that I should be
decently hiding myself away but I had the advantage of
being badly brought up and would not notice them.
I came in second in Ladies Shuffleboard but did badly at
partnered quoits despite being paired with a real athlete.
My partner was a man named Valentine who was one of
the two bowlers for the Jamaican cricket team and was
on his way home after having achieved, with the others, a
victory the month before at Lords, where they had beaten
England.
Lord Kitchener and Lord Beginner had written instant calypsos in honor of the victory.
"Those two little friends of mine

Ramadin and Valentine," went one of them. And here was the great Valentine himself, six feet four or five, thin as a rail, black as black, gentle and shy. He was the sort of man who must smile at his shoe and agree when the deck-games lady insisted.

Valentine and I made an incongruous pair.

"You look like a ball and bat," Axel told me.

A hurricane was in the vicinity and made the ship wallow the last day before its arrival in Kingston.

I was sitting in the upper lounge when the ship took one particularly high wave and every chair in the room with its back four-square to the downhill side fell over, including mine.

Axel and the stewardess were at my side before I could stand.

I lay on the floor laughing.

•   •   •

One thing made clear to me in the past year was that I had married a ladies' man. Whenever Axel went to help the hostess in the kitchen she would reappear with heightened color and a jollier disposition.

Axel thought of it as if he raised the value of the time passed. As if he were a social resource. As if he ranked along with the music and the drink.

I never thought the moon was made of green cheese, but then however much that's used to show an indecent credulity I was never *really* encouraged to believe it.

I was, on the other hand, encouraged by persons as diverse as Pearl Buck and Elsa Lanchester to believe that a man's sexual adrenalin deserves a support system.

Pearl Buck's books were all I would find to read when we would visit my grandmother in Santa Fe. Pearl Buck

had a variety of wonderful Number-One wives, each without flaw. In some instances it was wife Number-One who
chose her husband's wife Number-Two, making sure that
the younger woman would have a gentle disposition and
sweet breath.

Elsa Lanchester was a society wife in a movie that glit-
tered with cloth and jewels and attitudes. She told her
friends that she couldn't bear Reggie when he didn't have
a nice little flirtation going. He became too dull to talk to
and spoiled the look of the furniture.

In all the instances of these broad-minded women they
were only shown as charming and they were always the
most important woman present.

My own father would hit my mother with his fist whenever he wanted to; and when he had girlfriends my mother
suffered.

There was no doubt that Elsa Lanchester had it better.

Axel directed his interest toward the woman who sat in a
deck chair on the other side of my belly.

"Of course I love you!" she had just snapped at the small
girl who had come away from her toys to whisper in her
mother's ear.

The child shrank back from the anger in the woman's
voice and returned to shoving her toys about in a lack-
luster fashion. To please her mother the child pretended
to play.

"If I had *known* what a nuisance she would be without
her nurse…!"

The mother rolled her eyes up to show us that she had
suffered.

"You live in Jamaica?" Axel asked then.

"Yes," she smiled and was delighted to tell him, preening,
that she and her husband owned such-and-such a resort
in Montego Bay.

Axel's charm blossomed. And bore fruit.

"She wants us to visit," he told me after a turn around the deck with the lady in question while I and my book stayed at the deck chairs with the child and her toys.

Mrs. MacNeil had disappeared with her child to her appointment at the beauty salon below decks.

Now that her boredom was relieved by the presence of an attentive man she dazzled the other passengers nightly with a show of her various wardrobe and spent a piece of most afternoons laid up in the beauty salon for repairs and improvement.

The small girl also benefited by the woman's improved circumstance. She got an occasional pat and a smile. If she misjudged her mother's brief caress and clung to her the woman would recoil in a disgust equal to the child's longing. "She is *so* demanding!" The child would be shoved away.

During a desultory conversation the day before we were due to arrive Axel made the mistake that caused the lady to stop payment on his plans.
We were discussing whether it was cheaper for men or for women in their student years. Axel felt strongly that women were benefited by being taken to dinner by men.
"It might not be the case for unattractive women but any young woman with looks can count on getting a few free meals a week."

Mrs. MacNeil was concerned that we should both know she had also roughed it in her student days.
"When I was a student I lived on..." and she named some small amount, "... a week."
"That's my point exactly," Axel pounced, "and you were taken to dinner by your men friends!"

"Well, yes," she acknowledged.
"You could live that cheaply because you had your youth and good looks!" Axel said in triumph.
Mrs. MacNeil, freshly coiffed and draped round with peach chiffon to show off her figure, went frigid. She looked at Axel, who only knew he had made his point, and said "Well!"

"You said, 'that's when you *had* your *youth* and *good looks,*'" I explained, amazed that he still didn't understand what he had done.
"And so she had! That's why she could live so cheaply," he continued to insist.

• • •

The Caribbean is a deep valley with mountains that rise from the ocean floor to become Cuba, Haiti, Puerto Rico, a beaded line of the Bahamas, and Jamaica.
The ship sailed routinely among and through these mountain peaks, through the Windward Passage with Cuba closer on the right than Haiti, far off on the left, and continued dead straight for Jamaica, vivid green on a froth of lace where surf foamed.

Tropical air is a warm breathing, an intimacy, blind and nuzzling. It touches exposed skin with an unrelieved caress.

Valentine was not a man to swagger but his island home knew how to swagger for him, their own true darling.
On the dock three steel bands were set up and played with no reference to each other. All the dock was filled with dancing people.
The passengers had been told that no one might disembark until Valentine had been welcomed by the Lord Mayor.

Valentine flashed brief smiles upward but spent most of the welcoming speech looking at his shoe. The dignitaries melted in the heat and the Lord Mayor of Kingston, dressed for the occasion in a purple wool gown with a heavy gold chain of office hanging around his neck, gave Valentine a large golden key and proclaimed a public holiday.

Axel continued to scan the decks. He meant to reconcile himself with Mrs. MacNeil but she was nowhere to be seen.

As space opened, the crowd followed after Valentine and his greeters, and the other passengers made their way down the gangway.

Axel was met by two young men from the Kingston office of the Colonial Development Corporation who had made reservations for us at a hotel in the hills above Kingston. We had the use of a small Ford Prefect during the four days we meant to stay.

Axel was to meet with his business associates on Thursday morning and our plane to Belize was to leave on Friday.

Hibiscus too thick to see through, twelve feet high. Grass-green, fine as a thread to the thickness of a pencil, the most elegant lizard—"Isn't it charming! Oh look!"— caught and unmoving on the dining room wall next to a window that is almost to the ceiling and almost to the floor. No fear in that green shape against the white wall.

And us: we move in keeping with the place. Our gestures are larger and more languid. Ah, and the lizard is gone.

But it is raining a bit. And then it is raining more. And then it is not raining but high up there are lumps of cloud moving fast.

A warm breeze is blowing in gusts. At their worst the
gusts make the flowers rage and whip alongside the road. When the gust is past, the sun drops in a leaden thud from the sky.

It is a hurricane. Off there someplace there is a hurricane swirling its gigantic circle and snaking its influence over water... far enough away to give us only the side effects. So far.

"Hurricane."

"Hurricane?"

"Been around a couple of days now. Well off the island. North and East. Bit of a blow because of it."

"Is it likely to swing around and come here?"

"Warning flag's up to show it's within fifty miles. If the red flag goes up, that's when to head for cover. No real danger in all likelihood."

"Ah."

Two days later in the continuing uneven weather, drizzle and wind alternating with brilliant sunshine, we drove in the tiny Ford Prefect through Kingston enroute to the northern side of the island.

Axel meant to show me Montego Bay without Mrs. MacNeil's help.

Minutes after we had passed Government House the warning flag we hadn't noticed was lowered and a red flag was run up in its place.

Hurricane Lucille had changed her course and was moving toward Jamaica.

The car labored in its rise to three thousand feet above sea level. The windshield wipers were keyed to the engine. When the engine was not accelerating the wipers stopped. When we drove downhill, Axel had to open the car door and put his head out into the rain.

High up, at a view point, we stopped to look down into the valley. A lightning rod thirty feet away fulfilled its function. We were as shocked as if we had been hit. We were alive to register the shock. We made our way back to the car and continued on.

As we drove, the road was often awash with water and we drove into those washings with no sense of how deep they might be, trusting that the road was still there, out of eyesight.

We got to Tower Isle in the mid-afternoon. All the outdoors, the beach, the swimming pool, the outdoor dance floor, all was rain. To see what we had hoped for, we looked at the rack of picture postcards.

For company there were two couples of newlyweds on honeymoon who played canasta and told each other vivaciously about St. Louis, Missouri and Pocatello, Idaho.

All night the rain continued. The wind grew stronger, angling roughly, throwing the water in gusts by the bucket.

"The telephone wires are down," the desk clerk told us the next day, advising us against leaving the hotel. "Two touring buses that should have arrived this morning from Kingston have not come."

"If it gets too bad we'll come back," Axel answered.

"You do understand?" the desk clerk turned to me, giving up on Axel. "It is a hurricane."

"I have a business appointment tomorrow morning," Axel told him. "Our plane leaves day after tomorrow."

"I must advise you strongly against trying to cross the island," the clerk insisted.

"If it gets too bad we'll come back," Axel said again.

And with all the omnipotence of ignorance we left the hotel.

Axel had to drive with his head out of the door again.
Again we crossed the lakes of water that crossed the road.
Until we didn't.
One lake we drove into simply rose and continued to rise.
We sank into it.
When the water came through the floorboards Axel
switched the engine and headlights off and called, "You
take the wheel," to me.
He jumped out of the car and began to push. I reached
across to steer. The car sank deeper into water. The water
and mud was over my lap.
"Is the road washed away?" I yelled but couldn't be heard
above the racket of the storm.
The water lay on the road for fifty feet. Somewhere along
it the car began its uphill rise and rose out of its bath.

We stayed three days in a two-room cabin high on a hill
over a sugar cane field.
The overseer for what had been a banana plantation but
was now a wreckage of cane and banana trees and floating dead chickens and livestock had found us at our tem-
porary lake and invited us home. He lived with his wife
and two children in the small house.
What had been a hill was now a small island.
The third day the water began to recede and a man rode to
the house on a bicycle to say that a car had come through
from the island's other side by driving the coastal road.

We stopped twice and with others helped move a tree
from the road. The trees were still falling even though the
winds had passed. The landscape was ravaged, a chaos
of bits and breakage. Dead animals lay against whatever
barrier had stopped them.

The Kingston we returned to was changed.
Valentine had had his day and been blown off the front

page by accounts of the worst disaster to hit Jamaica in fifty years.

All the crops were ruined. The fields were destroyed. No planes could leave the island until the airstrips were cleared.

Axel found himself with time enough for his business meeting.

Another two days passed before we left.

Two photographs were taken of the mother-to-be during that week in Jamaica. The camera used was an old Zeiss-Eikon that leaked light streaks through the bellows.

In the first picture, taken the morning after arrival, it is early and she is standing outside her bedroom on a second-floor veranda. She is wearing a long nightgown of thin white stuff. Her body is a shadow through the cloth, a thin column swelling in the middle with the hidden presence of the unborn child. A slight breeze carries the gown and holds it against her.

She is not awkward.

She is standing in sunlight, looking out and down onto flowers.

Her body is an exquisite curving.

She saw a large expanse of clipped grass, its periphery defined by a tall hedge of pinkish-red hibiscus, the flower large with ragged edges and a single pistil, thin and golden, protruding into the air. She saw an unused fountain half-filled with a clutter of dry leaves and debris. The metal pipe in the center was rusted and dribbled a constant wavery bit of water. At night frogs congregated in that dampness and sounded their racket.

In the later photograph, after the hurricane has turned on its track and returned to wreck the island, she is at the airport.

Now she is awkward, her bulk looking as if the storm has left her stranded. She is frowning and tired.

Our next stop would be an arrival at our future.

In The Colony

The town is mainly flat, much of it on land reclaimed from swamp. It is cut into two parts by a narrow river which widens at its mouth into a bay, a natural harbor. Queen Street, the main street of the town, crosses the river with a metal bridge. A bridge is lifted twice during the day to let fishing boats go through. The first time at dawn when the boats must go out. The second time in the early evening when they return.

The houses are of two kinds with variations. The "local" house is small and square, one story near or on the ground, square holes for windows with solid flats of wood hinged at the top to be propped open in the day time and closed at night with a latch. These houses are made of soft wood and often lean in the direction that is most eaten away. The second type of house is hardwood, painted white. It is two stories raised still higher on a foundation of stilts for more breeze and fewer mosquitoes. The high-pitched roof is corrugated tin painted red to slow the inevitable rust. Around the roof's edge is a tin gutter to catch rainfall. A pipe extends from the gutter to an enormous round water tank that sits in the yard as companion piece to the houses that can afford it. This second kind of house commands the major streets, the pleasant views, the sea breezes. This is the "backra" house where the white people live.

One of these houses with a small square of grass in front sat among others on the Foreshore. It faced, across a paved road, the ocean and the moorings of half a dozen small sailing boats owned by people who sailed for pleasure.
Quin Culpe, thin and bony, dressed in white kit for tennis at the club, wandered musing into the downstairs bedroom of his company-supplied home.
He wondered, as all do who like to cut it sharp, whether he might have asked for more money. He had asked for twice what they would have paid at the boarding house.
Not too dear a price, he thought. Generous in fact for a man who loved his home and privacy. Generous of him to give up a bit of his well-loved home to strangers. A friend in need.
He stood in the uninteresting room to see it anew.
Perfectly adequate, he thought.
It occurred to him that he could ask for more money after the baby came. It would be more work for the cook and the maid. Bottles and nappies.
He sniffed a sniff with a nose as pointed as any bird that ever feathered its nest and went off on his two legs to his car.
He was proud of his legs.
He thought of himself as small but shapely.

Racquet and tennis balls were in the back seat and without any particular farewell to his wife, giving her no chance

to remind him that today was the day for her weekly visit
to the prenatal clinic (My God! two pregnant women in
one small house! Now *that* was above and beyond the call
of duty!) he climbed into his tidy blue Morris Minor and
reversed out of the driveway.
The walk would be good for her.
They must both stay fit.
He'd be the first to say that she should take a taxi, but he
knew that she would walk. He was an indulgent husband
with a decently thrifty wife. He would chide her for her
little economies. She was never egged on by his chiding to
reckless expenditure.

In this tropical place the books will fall away from their
bindings if they are not taken regularly from their shelves
and exposed to light. Dark clothing must be taken regularly from the closet and hung in the day's air or it will
develop splotches of mildew.
Shoes not worn regularly grow moss inside.

"Lice! Lice! Trow de bahl! Trow de bahl, Lice!"
Children are playing in a vacant lot near the Foreshore.
The girl named Lois throws the ball.

Water must be boiled, cooled and bottled for drinking.
Mosquito nets circle the beds.
The buzzards of this place, John Crow their local name,
wheel slowly through the hot skies on the lookout for
carrion.

Still, it would be strange (Quin Culpe drove around a
sleeping dog) to have foreigners in the house. God knows
what they might expect. Danes are notorious feeders
and all the world knows how Americans are. Americans
clamor in the marketplaces of the world, buying, buying,
greedy, voracious. They would ruin him if they could.

He must be quite firm. They would find him a man to be reckoned with. Their standards would soar no higher than his well-ordered English household was prepared to sustain.

I looked at all that green smashed to garbage, poor little paradise.

The major news that morning had been how many nations were coming running with the green stuff that would kiss it and make it well.

The local plane, rattling and small, with one propeller, took us away from what would never be included in a tourist brochure.

Travel made me tired.
I wanted my body back.
I wanted to be the only person inside my skin.
I was at the end of my rope and we'd finally arrived at the beginning.

The Belize airport building shimmered in the heat to show it was apt to disappear, a plastered-over flat box with WELCOME TO BRITISH HONDURAS painted on the front.
Leaving the plane, walking on soft tar, the passengers shoved through solid heat on their energyless way to a door marked Immigration.
Past Immigration and Customs the building was cool. We were handed iced fruit drinks by Mr. Sinclair as we left the railed enclosure.
We also met Mr. Culpe who moved constantly and never stopped smiling.
We all shook hands.
Mr. Sinclair had thick gray hair and freckles, was middle-aged, friendly. He arranged for our bags to be put in his car and we waited inside while it was being done.

The weekly plane from Jamaica and the weekly plane from New Orleans both arrived the same day; the first at 1:00 PM, the second at 3:00 PM. Anyone arriving or

leaving from the colony would be at the airport together
with whoever had come to say goodbye or hello or both.
Rob Sinclair and Quin Culpe knew everyone. They knew
others who had arrived and those who had come to meet
them and knew the passengers checking their bags for the
return flight to Kingston and knew who was waiting to
meet whom on the New Orleans flight.
"Allan! Good to see you. You're on your way to the States?"
Everyone here seemed to know everyone else's business.
And there were people who had simply come out for the
weekly party this all made.

"You know how it is in the tropics," Rob said over his
shoulder to Axel. The thin road was leading us out of the
airport past bushes of dusty hibiscus.
He meant that we had no house.
Axel agreed. Oh yes, he was all too well aware of how
plans and execution were at cross purposes in the tropics.
"It might be as long as two months, but in the meantime
Quin and Mavis have offered to house you. The CDC will
pay for it."
"How generous of you," I said over my own shoulder to
Quin Culpe.
"It's nothing fancy but I think you'll be comfortable."

Some people move around the world like they're normal
because that's what passes for human style but really
they're like black holes in the Universe. There's a ravenous
desire inside them that sucks and sucks and can't ever be
content. They can't bear anybody else's reality.
Whatever and whoever comes into prolonged contact
with a neurotic runs the risk and likelihood of some kind
of transformation.
Ideally you see it in them, what they are, fast enough to let
you go into rapid reverse and back out.
In this instance we didn't know Quin Culpe and we had

been promised to him for a couple of months.
That's all. It wasn't forever. Just a couple of months.

"What hit me," people say, walking away in a daze after just five minutes with a potent neurotic.
Just a couple of months.
And that "couple of months" was the next plan in a system of plans that had already let us down. You know how it is in the tropics.

"MY DARLING ROSE," I said to Rob Sinclair, pointing. Between the airport and Belize the road was one lane of tartop. There were passing bays at regular intervals. The road went through lightweight jungle, walls of growth on both sides fifteen feet high; and through swamp where the water was the rich color of oil, and white lilies floated on the surface. Iguanas sunned on fallen logs. We would sometimes catch sight of an orchid, a sudden color, in the crotch of a tree far enough off the road so it hadn't fallen an easy prey to the passing traffic.

MY OWN
HEARTS DESIRE

The houses along the way to the town were named. The names were written in paint on board or on a rusting piece of corrugated tin, and nailed onto posts or trees near the road. The houses were shanties made of wood with a door and two windows. The names were a high-flown fancy. One, surrounded by flowers, leaning sideways, ready to fall, was MODERN TIMES.

On the outskirts of the town the shanties multiplied rapidly, became a swarming of wooden structures and half-naked children and thin sick-looking dogs. A smell rose from a nearby canal.

It was the place where the nighttime and maybe daytime slop jars were emptied. When a pail was emptied there would be a swirl in the water.

If you didn't know and reached in you might well lose a finger.

There was always the heat.

The ocean breezes never reached these back streets. Children and chickens and dogs; one dog that had run out of luck was a feast for half a dozen buzzards. They racketed and hissed at each other but were too engrossed in feeding to fight. They hopped over and around the ragged carcass with their wings out for balance.

Ugly.

Ugly.

We swung right onto what Rob Sinclair said was Queen Street, crossed a metal bridge. Passed the market.

The market was slow and bright with cloths stretched to make shade over the fruits and vegetables and chilis. We turned toward the foreshore and came, at last, on a sweet ocean breeze that carried the smell of salt into the car and cooled us.

"Not fancy, but I think you will find it comfortable." Quin Culpe repeated his formula as we stood in the center of a drab and barren room.

Ah, but the front window looked onto the ocean and the boats moored there, and would show the sunset.

It *was* only two months.

''I'm sure we'll be comfortable," Axel reassured him.

Rob Sinclair looked the room over more critically. When he and his wife had come to dinner this had been the room where the guests had left their wraps. He distinctly remembered more furniture. There had been another bedside

table, another lamp, a small desk with a straight chair.
Some pictures, landscapes, fruit, something like that.
"If there's anything you need we can get it at the office.
We've got the furniture, some of it, for your house. You
can take any of it you'd like and then take it along with
you when you leave."
He saw no point in pushing the issue.

Axel wanted a drafting table. He liked to bring work
home. And yes, I'd like a soft chair. Something I could
sit in next to the window when I wanted to sit and read.

Quin Culpe felt a revulsion at the instant demands until
he remembered that he wanted the two of them to stay in
their room as much as possible.
"Working evenings, eh?" he smiled approvingly. "You'll
make the rest of us look like lay-abouts."
"Oh, Quin," his wife said breathlessly, "no one could
think that about *you!* You're never home before six and
you often go back."
Mrs. Culpe was Mavis. "Do call me Mavis!" she had
insisted.
Mavis hovered in the doorway, perpetually on the verge
of leaving the room. Her husband made no response to
her endorsement.

"Is there a particular time of day for paying our respects
at Government House?" Axel asked.
Quin Culpe stopped himself short of saying that as for-
eigners they would not be expected.
"Oh no. Anytime between ten and four. You'll meet Sir
Arthur's secretary, Mr. Niles. He'll have the book."
Quin Culpe thought Axel was being pushy.
The form was, one signed the book, then got asked to din-
ner or at least to tea. Axel was simply asking to be asked.

I wondered whether Quin Culpe might be shy with
strangers.
His wife certainly was, hanging in the doorway.
How could I know that in our host we had the town's de-
mon of the dance floor, the whirlwind of the tennis courts,
the prince of style.

Rob Sinclair invited the four of us to dinner the following
night and left.
Mavis asked whether anyone would like tea.

"Heavenly Prospect," I answered, signs in my mind.

Roosters bring the day up, poor scrawny things to sound
so splendid. Before the first show of light their racket begins. They excite each other to hysterical effort. The dogs
are also infected, that in the day's heat will have as much
as they can do to move from the sun into the shade. They
bark and howl until they feel they've done enough.

Old Vivvy, wearing a dirty rainbow of dresses, goes into
Mrs. MacDougal's prized garden, a shadow among early
dawn shadows, to pick the flowers.
"When that woman was a child everything she touched
was gold!"
"When that woman was a child..." she owned the first
piano in the colony. Her parents meant to make her a
concert pianist. Both parents were killed in an accident
and the child's guardian took the money. That was the
story.
In the local voice, a calypso swing to her speech and
with the drawn out, pulled out rhythms of any storyteller
dealing with a myth, Rosa told me (later),"Whan dhat
whomahn wass a chile *ehverting* she touch wass ghol!"
Who stands now in the palest gray lift of early morning at
Mrs. MacDougal's door, a mahogany door polished to a
high shine, and drops the brass knocker repeatedly on its
sounding brass panel until the door is opened a cautious
crack then wide by Mrs. MacDougal herself, in a pink
dressing gown, who looks in shock to see her treasured
darlings, all the flowers from her garden, in a crushed
mass, a madwoman's bouquet, held toward her as Old
Vivvy simpering says "Fi' cents?"
Mrs. MacDougal pays the five cents and brings her
fresh-picked flowers indoors, to the kitchen, where she
puts water in the sink and the flowers also. Flowers, she
would be the first to say, are best picked in the early
morning while dew still clings to the petals, as it does
to these.

Vivvy takes her five cents and turns down Queen Street to go to the market.

In the gray light of pre-sunrise the fishing boats are still arriving to unload. Donkey carts filled with small stringy avocados, juiceless oranges, pineapples, breadfruit, plantain, coconuts, are standing around in the bare yard. At the yard's far end are boxes of wilted chickens. Iguanas scuffle in the dirt, their front legs pulled like arms to be tied behind their backs.

"Dey are de *bess* ting in de whorl to eat!" Rosa would insist to me who never, all the time I was there, did eat one. There is an inner building where half-carcasses hang, blood dripping, and flies and cats go through the mesh to feed on the meat.

Mrs. MacDougal leaves the flowers in the sink until later and returns to her bed up the polished winding staircase. Her house is graceful throughout, the advantage of her own and Gordon's taste. On the second floor she passes the door to Gordon's bedroom, the door to her dying husband's bedroom, and enters her own bedroom, a feminine haven of imported goods.

She has a headache beginning that will last, probably, all day, a fierce headache. All her flowers have been picked and having them in the kitchen sink in the water is no help at all.

The rising sun finds the day well under way in that small
colony of houses.

"You gwan to cahtch you a husbahn foh suah, you keep
lookin lahk dhat!" a woman almost hidden by trays of
green and yellow chili peppers called out to Sally, the
Culpe's cook, as she passed with her meager basket.

Sally's bad-temper was settled enough to not be relieved
by the laughter around her, by the voices singing and call-
ing over the large market space.

"Yes, indeed," another woman took up the joke and sang,
"You wahnt to be happy an' live a king's life never make
a pretty wohmahn your wife..."

Sour-faced Sally walked on past, down the long aisle
of breadfruit and avocados, to the quayside where she
bought a red snapper for dinner. Marketing would be even
less a pleasure now. Mr. Culpe had made it clear that she
would not have more money for the two extra lodgers.

She walked back through the shaded meat house and out
through the poultry yard to Queen Street, turned left and
left again and was on the cobbled road that ran along the
Foreshore and would take her to her morning's work.

The roosters have crowed and stopped. The dogs have
barked and stopped. Mrs. MacDougal is back in her bed
asleep, a damp cloth on her forehead. Old Vivvy, having
been raised to be clean, comes to the Fort Square seawall
to bathe. The cast-off dresses she wears in layers of filthy
faded print are laid over the wall.

Wearing, on different mornings, one dress or two or nothing
at all, she goes into the water among the morning's slops.

Light pours horizontally over the flat still water and the
day's heat begins.

On the Foreshore a battle had begun: the battle of the
breakfast egg.

Quin Culpe had begun as he meant to continue.

"Fried bread and marmalade is perfectly adequate," he insisted to Sally, who stared resentfully at the floor.

"But Quin," Mavis Culpe quavered, hearing the echo of the notices given by all the cooks before this one, "we have *always* had eggs for breakfast!"

"There's no need for a feast at breakfast time!" Quin Culpe's eyes bulged with pressure.

His hair was glued to his head, the curl caught and held like a tightly plowed field above the fierce wrinkles on his forehead above the intent beak of his nose. If the world could only be held in place and controlled so simply.

"Our food bills have gone up!" he said to his wife.

He turned to the couple who must sit through this early morning tirade with a most inappropriate smile wavering on his mouth.

He meant them to see that he was not unreasonable.

"There've been many times in my life when I would have thought myself lucky to have had a cup of tea, much less fried bread and homemade jam!" He named off the items as if he named jewels.

We looked back at him, not to be fooled.

This breakfast time hysteria of Quin's had shocked us both.

"You know, Quin, we *can* stay at the boarding house. It would cost the CDC less money and we wouldn't be inconveniencing anyone."

Quin Culpe had counted on good manners. The manners his wife and daughter used quite normally in their dealings with him. It had not occurred to him that the Raasloffs might simply leave if the situation didn't suit them.

Now he must flush a red color and assure us that the last thing he wanted was for us to leave.

He had hoped that the thirty dollars a day he was being
paid would all be profit. He acknowledged our presence
and our demands to the extent of giving Sally another two
dollars a day for her marketing.

• • •

As boarders we were quickly privy to the inner workings
of the Culpe household. We were the first persons ever to
be given the benefit of being, as Quin Culpe told us, smiling, just prior to one of his ongoing attempts to deprive
us of food or furniture or the use of the living room, "a
part of the family."
We didn't want it, this "benefit."
It wasn't the description in any case but the *reason* for it,
our *presence*, that made us know more than we wanted
to know.

As we were introduced into the Colony we saw that the
general sense held of Quin Culpe was that he was a gal-
lant, a devil with the ladies on the dance floor, always up
for a good game of tennis; in short, a social asset in this
place where people made their own entertainment.

Mavis Culpe was a dry stick who took alarm whenever
she was made public, shy to the point of being backward.
When she was elsewhere than her own home for tea and
was offered a choice of pastries her voice would trail away
to nothing as she said, "Oh, I really shouldn't…"
Her gesture, even as she reached for a small cake on the
offered tray, would falter as if she meant to draw back.
Her hostess would wait, knowing Mavis to be a hesita-
tor, and a cake would be chosen, would be grasped, and
would waver its way into Mavis Culpe's limbo.

She might have been different without Quin to recite a nightly litany of her public shortcomings.

''Then you...'' we would hear his voice in the darkened house.

"And then you..." his bookkeeper's mind clicking and tabulating.

His voice came down through the ceiling into our bedroom. He went on and on.

Quin Culpe encouraged his daughter to despise her mother as he did.

There was a nightly drama of Virginia's bedtime.

"It's your bedtime, darling," Mavis would be pleading from the start.

Virginia would look at her father.

He would read his paper.

He would pay no attention.

"Go upstairs, dear, and put on your nighty."

Virginia's father would not look up until she rose grudgingly to her feet and began to make her way to the stairs.

"Well, sweetheart, I haven't given you any time today. Come over and sit on my lap."

"Oh, Quin," Mavis would say.

The daughter, Virginia, was large for her age and overhealthy, like a child movie-star. She hovered, with her large head and sausage curls, at the edge of her personal lighted stage. At any moment the music might begin.

Larger than Shirley Temple in her heyday and without the range of Hollywood, she was reduced to such second-rate ploys as standing in the middle of the room when her mother had ladies visiting, batting her eyelashes, and saying in ringing baby tones, "Oh! I made a mistook!"

Her mother would say tiredly, "There, dear, do go and play."

She was larger than her father, the healthy, hefty child sitting on his thin legs. She was larger than her father, larger than her mother, larger than the house, triumphant.
And her father was a sharp-faced little animal peering around a corner of her, his teeth bared in a grin. The two of them looked at Mavis, who stood with a smile catching and losing the outside corners of her mouth.

The hotel was to be built on reclaimed land.

The land could not hold the weight of the proposed building.

The weight of the building would cause it to slowly sink into the ground.

Axel and the chief engineer walked over the site, blueprints in hand.

This was the land and here was the first problem.

"Doesn't register a thing!" Mavis whispered in my ear. "Not a thing!"

She moved nearer the platform where the old man sat behind a desk, his eyes overlooking his store, where everything necessary to civilized life could be found. She trilled, "Hello, Mr. MacDougal!"

He looked down at us. I don't think he recognized Mavis but that must have been a common experience for him. When the world caught his attention it knew him, who he was, where he was. He smiled.

He was angelic, the innocence of his smile.

"And there's Gordon!"

Mavis loved having me in tow. She would introduce me to someone with a nervous flurry, a busyness.

Gordon was young and sturdy. He wore a blue shirt with a white collar. He longed for Paris and London. He sat on the platform beside his father and drew line drawings of Marlene Dietrich.

He was my dear friend.

He said to me about Zaydie, when she didn't accept an invitation to come sailing, "She thinks you mean to push her overboard!"

Of course she wouldn't come.

Not even to pull the wool over Alicia's eyes.

When Axel met Zaydie one reason she kept him at arm's

length, or so he told me, was because she was already having an affair with Alicia's husband, Pawli.

Pawli was head surgeon at the hospital where Zaydie was a nurse.

It was the only hospital and therefore it was the hospital where I had gone to have my daughter.

Axel met Zaydie during his visits to me there.

I met Alicia when I took a length of gray silk crepe to my dressmaker to be made into the dress and hat I would wear at Government House at the garden party for the Queen's birthday.

By that time Alicia had heard about Axel from Pawli. Pawli had told his wife at length about the architect who was romancing his nurse.

Alicia and I immediately liked each other.

She did what she could to protect me from Axel's woman-izing; that is she never mentioned it except to imply that he only flirted.

And I protected her the same way.

I didn't ever tell her that she was hearing so much from her husband because he was covering his own traces.

I had my own idea of how it was and I adhered to it. Elsa Lanchester and I just loved it when Axel had a nice little flirtation going.

It made him so cheerful.

Alicia knew more about me than I did.

I felt it more than I could acknowledge. It would have taken a whole new theory for that shift.

At the least pang I would retreat to that prepared place.

I wouldn't have pushed Zaydie overboard.

I would have been enclosed in my own little functioning idea.

The bed had an iron frame painted white with footrails rising high enough to hold a small metal box on hooks. In that white box, swaddled in soft blankets, was my daughter. If she fussed I could stretch my leg and rock her iron cradle with my toe.

My stomach was cramping, stitches in my tender parts were made of catgut and rapidly drying to needles but I felt fine.

I was ahead of the schedule, precocious; only twenty and already a completed item.

Here's myself, set to go dancing, there's the infant, there comes the husband bringing flowers.

One of the things the mind does is give us in our head what we'll never have in our hands.

If the line of thought is high-minded we think we're idealistic. If it's wanting a million dollars it's only what would be ideal. In either case the real gets trashed, or at least bruised.

At the most wonderful moment someone can say, "Now this would really be perfect if only…" and the projection slides into place adjacent to what only a moment before was as good as it could be.

What passes for idealism is often nothing more than a lousy mental habit.

And sometimes what passes for idealism is more like: it-takes-all-the-encouragement-we-can-imagine-just-to-face-the-day.

Usually it's an almighty mix and medley of all of the above plus more.

When Axel showed up as my loophole in a tattered condition I didn't see myself as ruined and on the run. I saw myself as an artist enroute. Things like Axel happen to people like artists, who lead full and interesting lives. There was something akin to idealism in my belief that I deserved it, however unlikely.

I left home so my presumptions could be aspirations.

I never recovered from the social change and the leg up
that marriage gave me.
When I think that marrying Axel displaced me I have to
remember just how displaced I was when we met.
I was capable of being married by an FBI agent and thinking I knew what was going on.

Lying in my "private room," a partitioned-off bit at the
end of the barracks room that was the hospital's maternity
ward, rocking my daughter's cradle, a sea breeze through
the window, the future I perpetually day-dreamed had
shrunk to the immediate and the possible.

• • •

The baby was asleep in the house and Axel and I sat on
the seawall.
The blue sky tended to mauve with the sunset, became a
darker pink shot with orange, became a pinked purple as
oncoming night shifted the balance. Through it all the still
water reflected the changes, merging with the horizon to
make it disappear. The sky passed overhead, curved and
returned to lap at the wall where we sat. Boats and moor-
ing posts were strokes of black and floated in mid-air. A
pelican threw itself in a downward fall, head first, into the
darkening mauve of the water, somersaulted and bobbed
there, its long beak pointed to heaven while it swallowed.

There was, briefly, before the advent of Zaydie, a period
of fruition, an enjoyment and sense of well-being that bor-
dered on delight. A blissful state that love, given all the
modern domestic ramifications, might be.

Quin came from the kitchen holding a plate in each hand.
"Welsh Rarebit!" he announced and returned to the kitch-
en for more plates.

The plates held a single piece of fried bread with cheese melted over the top.

Quin's tone of voice as he extolled the delights of Welsh Rarebit was the voice adults use with children to make a murky fact seem joyous and acceptable.

"*Lovely* carrots!" Mothers say to con their infants.

Very well then, Welsh Rarebit.

Three of the adults at the table ate heartily. Without fanfare we finished our piece of bread and cheese in about six bites, only to see that Quin was making a project of his. He manipulated his cutlery as if he were about a more complex business. He took minute bites and savored each bite.

When he saw us sitting as if we waited, which we were doing, he said, "The cook is washing up."

"I can get more for myself. She needn't be bothered," and I stood with my plate in hand.

"Oh no!" Quin's mind flashed panic. He had gone to great lengths to convince the Raasloffs that Sally would not tolerate anyone in her kitchen. He meant to keep them on strict rations if he could manage it. No casual evening snacking.

"I *can* ask her to make more," he said.

His face was hurt with the unfairness of it. He was outraged by the greed but in all decency must conceal it. His face twitched.

No one had realized there was no more.

Now it was obvious.

It was meant to be a coup.

"Yes, thank you," Axel said. "We would like more. And perhaps some fruit."

I still stood holding my empty plate.

Dickens in the tropics.

"Would anyone else care for more?" Quin castigated himself.

Mavis insisted that she was quite content, thank you.

"That was quite enough for me. Quite enough," she babbled.

Quin's glare, which seemed to say that hanging would have been good enough for her, shut her up. He left off glaring before she could misunderstand and think he wanted her to want more.

I once heard Quin describing the room he rented to us. We were all out to dinner, which happened, fortunately, often. He made our bedroom sound as if it were an excursion tour to exotic places. Directly on the water with fishing boats and the sunset laid on. He stopped short at nightly dancing in the ballroom.

"He wasn't always like this," Mavis told me one morning. She hated it that Quin so exposed himself at home and we were there to see it. She would rather be thought dull than pathetic.

Quin Culpe had received a letter in the morning mail.
He sat holding it and went into a kind of trance.
He sat and continued reading one page of the letter.
Time passed.
An hour passed and he sat reading his page.
In fact he was not reading. After this first time I often saw him caught in this same catatonia.
Mavis came into the bedroom where I was and wept.

"He was the most gentle man I ever knew. But they took him prisoner and when he came home he was like he is now."

It was worse than she could say. Faded and desperate, she was weighed down to the insignificance of a third rate charwoman by her self-centered undersize husband and her vivacious oversize daughter. Her voice was a whining

whisper. Her highest hope was to be overlooked. It was
made more bearable by an explanation. She was not a
victim of her husband. She was, with so many others, a
victim of the war.

Perhaps, equally possible, he *had* been gentle, caught in
that brief flare of romance, the wartime honeymoon the
couple had had.
Then, returned after the war, he became himself again.
The honeymoon is over.
Returned home, did his altered being content him?
Was it as satisfying for him to make his wife miserable as
it had been to make her happy?

Was it, simply, the same?
An equation of the emotions: X is to Y as A is to B.

• • •

Quin Culpe didn't matter as much as these pages have
made him seem.
The memories I have of him are bombastic and demanding, as he was.
It's often the case that bombast wins.
The rest of us desperately invent Democracy and fair play
and such like overviews to slow the despots down.

There was one last incident from that time in that house.
I heard Mavis cry out in pain and came out of my bedroom to find her doubled over, holding the bulk of her
belly in both arms.
On the stairs above her Virginia stood, triumphant.
She looked at me, the unexpected observer, with a hatred
totally unchildlike. Her curls and face combined to make
a Medusa mask.
"I tripped on the stairs," Mavis gasped to me, her face white.

"I fell against the...," and she looked around for something hard to have fallen against.
"Sit down. Let me get you some tea," and I helped her to
the couch, tucked an afghan around her.
All three of us knew that Virginia had kicked her.

"You're not supposed to go in the kitchen!" Virginia spat
while I put water to boil and took down a brown earth-
enware teapot.
"That's the teapot for *Sally!*" the child glared. "*I'm* not
going to drink any tea made in *that* pot!"

When the tea had brewed I poured milk in a cup, poured
tea, added sugar, gave it to Mavis.

· · ·

For three months, of necessity, we shared that house. We
would have been there another three months if Axel had
not seen our own house through its building. When he
visited it and saw how far behind it was, saw the quality
of the help, he insisted; and Mr. Sinclair, who was perhaps not all that unknowledgeable concerning the Culpes,
agreed that it needed to be pushed along.

In any case the hotel was being drastically delayed by the
newest plan to drive reinforced concrete pilings into the
reclaimed land as a solution to its instability. The rods
that were to be the reinforcement must be shipped from
England.
So Axel did have the time.

The house was finished and we moved into it.
Just that half mile was enough to shrink Quin Culpe to
lifesize and Mavis to a distant domestic tragedy.

The club.
Government House.
The American Consulate.
The market.
The airport.
The length of Queen Street.
All the private houses.

All in the same land locked showboat.

All the plots, however small, had a beginning, middle, and end.
As the American couple who hired Ethel Golong for a cook.
She was a witch but they were too intelligent to believe in such things. Thin and bent with a bandanna tied hard around her head and an evil glare, she shuffled and muttered spells as she worked around in their house. Which they ignored, not wanting to embarrass her.
To eat a meal at their house—the food was unbelievably bad—was to come under Ethel Golong's evil eye.
They fired her at last and she laid down an obeah so powerful that no one in the colony would work for them.

For some time the blond pants-suited wife was at the market by six to do her day's shopping. She did her laundry by hand.
They began to find little bags of bones and rubbish on the doorstep. When the bags moved into the house and under the pillows on their bed they appealed to the police.

It was as good as a public holiday, I heard, the day two sturdy young policemen, immaculate in starched khaki, dragged the old woman to the house and with an audience of silent spectators, her eyes walling in all directions, she removed the obeah.

On the second-floor veranda of the house across the street
the two Delara girls and their mother had begun their day
of slow rocking in the shade. Each was equipped with a
rocking chair, a fan, and a glass of iced fruit juice.

The hotel manager, who was prematurely hired by the
CDC and now had at the least two years of time on his
hands, with salary, had begun to court the elder of the
Delara girls.

The two girls had been kept drastically intact their whole
lives against just such a possibility.

The manager was given a plan of behavior that must be
adhered to.
His conduct was one side of a transaction. The other side
was this young woman's guaranteed condition. She was
untouched. She had never even been to a dance. She had
never walked on the street without the company of her
mother or her father.

The suitor found himself dancing a very courtly dance
indeed.
He had to make a daily call in the cool of the afternoon
and sit on the veranda with his beloved and her sister and
her mother.
When the father came onto the porch the suitor would
rise, shake hands all around and leave.
Two times a week he was invited to stay to dinner.
He brought flowers daily and candy for the mother on the
days he stayed to dinner.

He sometimes sailed with us and we asked him every
question we could think of apropos his wooing. Between

Axel and myself we asked everything.
He answered every question as well as he could. He had
no compunction, no feeling of sacred privacy. That deli-
cacy must have been used up in the actuality.

He was fascinated.
He had never in his life met a virgin with a guarantee.
The eroticism inherent in that daily prospectus was more
than he had ever known.
It seemed that the two years he had would be just about
what he needed to bring so intricate a courtship to its
happy resolution.

•   •   •

I put on dark glasses, took up my basket, went down the
stairs to pass underneath the house. It was cool there and
dark, with the slight sharp sound of mosquitoes.
I said good-morning to Rosa where she washed clothes.
She came daily to wash what had been dirtied since the
day before and iron what she had washed the day before.

I walked onto the bright street.
The sky was as high as the sun.
Through all that distance the heat fell to ripple on the
cement sidewalk.
The Delaras looked down, watched me along the street.
The street was their daily theater.
I wondered whether, in their scheme of things, it was in-
decent even for a married woman to walk out alone.
Probably it was.

"Must be quite a change for you, eh, Mrs. Raasloff, this
weather?"
"Oh, it's very hot and dry where I come from, Sir John."
Sir John continued on past yard goods where I was

choosing enough gray silk crepe for a dress and to cover a hat.

"Morning, Mr. MacDougal! Morning, Gordon!"

He gives them the same slight salute he has given me.

Mr. MacDougal gives Sir John's unseeing back the same nod and sweet smile he dispenses to all who pass. He is unable to distinguish between his customers and his employees and his old friends.

Monday through Friday he is "at work."

He sits, mildly gazing from his chair, on the platform that lets him overlook the store.

He is becoming transparent. The color is fading from his skin and his hair. His eyes are a blue so pale it's as if the sky shows through his head.

He is driven to the store every morning by a chauffeur. He is driven home at midday.

Gordon always walked.

Mr. MacDougal didn't want to stay home afternoons but his strength failed him.

He didn't come to work one morning because he had died the night before.

Gordon's mother, Ivy, needed Gordon at home evenings. She could bear his going to the store in the daytime but he must be home at night.

And Gordon also began to fade.

Of course he was saddened by his father's death; but he was devastated by his mother's demands.

Now that Mr. MacDougal was not there to spoil the projection, she meant that she and Gordon would share a delightful household forever.

She expected to be invited wherever Gordon was invited as if she were his wife. Often it was not appropriate or the hosts didn't realize she felt as she did and Gordon would be invited on his own.

Many times he didn't go. He went only when it mattered to him so much that he would face his mother's reproach.

I would visit him at the store and we would plot ways to get him out of the house so his mother would be left feeling the least breach of trust.

I am not talking about the time immediately after his father's death.

I am talking about months later.

Ivy realized that our house was where Gordon might often end up, whatever his righteous errand had been. She suspected he came to our house and enjoyed himself.

She would telephone us and ask to speak to him. Sometimes he was with us and sometimes he wasn't. Since she waited up for him the calls could come as late as two in the morning.

The telephone would ring in the dark living room.

The baby would wake and begin to cry.

One of us would fight our way through the mosquito net that surrounded our bed at night and make our way to the telephone, knowing it would be Ivy MacDougal. There was no hope that she would hang up first if we let the telephone ring.

It was a way she punished us for giving Gordon another place to be than home.

A long afternoon.

All the time in the world.

The flowering lane opens out and we have been brought to the heart of the camp. Barracks buildings spread out

over an expanse of flat ground. They are beautified by
plantings of croton and bougainvillea and the perpetual
orange-red hibiscus.
Inside one of the buildings voices rise and fall.

"...just when the cook brought it in she dropped it.
A whole turkey! It simply slithered off the platter and
bounced along the floor. We were stunned! I had *no* idea
of what to do. The *Governor*! *And* Sir John and Lady
Agatha. I had *nothing* else I could feed them! *Then* the
cook said, "Should I take this turkey back to the kitchen,
Ma'am, and bring the *other* turkey in?"

"...this beastly crowd... "

"How *does* one avoid hearing the story of the 1930 hurricane from Mr. Frazier?"
"One avoids Mr. Frazier."

A long afternoon into a long evening. Dinner and dancing.
Does it sound trivial?
A useless and airy waste?
It was more than vanity and a lack of purpose that made
me love it.
I was in the right place in the nick of time.

• • •

What mattered was the entirety.
For the first time in my life I felt secure and acceptable,
the faults covered over. I believed it too, that I had arrived
at my "true" person, I was sweet-natured, young, a good
dancer; I was someone I could live with.
Being with Axel had given me this, and my suffusion of
contentment was love, in my imagination.
I never trembled because I'd see him in the next moment.

But marriage precludes that tremble in any event, doesn't it? Even for the most impassioned, doesn't constant proximity do that tremble in?

"But I wanted *more!* I wanted *more!*" is wailing in my head back of this rationale.

It was all much as Axel had proposed it would be. And I was apparently all he had hoped.

But what mattered was the entirety.
For the first time in my life the vocabulary I had got from books and the vocabulary I used in conversation meshed. That's not trivial.
And I saw a variety of women, all unique and, with Mavis the exception, articulate. They all, with Mavis the exception, led forthright lives.
And all the stories were overt.
That *does* reduce the isolation.

•   •   •

At the far end of the room the Sergeant-Major is singing. *"Ahnd it's awlroit in the summertoim ... In the summertoim it's LOVERLY ... Whoil me old man's paintin 'ard ... Oim posin in the old backyard ..."*
The Sergeant-Major is feeling no pain and is a hit.
"Isn't it a silly shame that Sergeant-Majors aren't issued a decent dress uniform?" Richard, the dark-haired subaltern asks.
"I didn't know they weren't."
"They have to wear *that!*"
The Sergeant-Major is wearing freshly washed, starched and pressed khaki, a tunic, and tropical issue shorts. He seems untouched by any sense of being among the peacocks though it is true that the commissioned officers all wear black dress trousers with a satin stripe down the

side, a white dress shirt, white mess jacket and red cum-
merbund, and are very dashing.
"Babies, wet behind the ears," Richard says, "nineteen
and twenty years old. They're given a commission because
of the school they've gone to and they're sent out to order
troops about. Well, *that's* the man that keeps them from
making bloody fools of themselves. He makes them look
good in front of the men, makes them look like officers!"

The Sergeant-Major's wife is smiling, large-bodied,
comfortable.
She likes it that he has this turn in him.
She is as quiet as the chair she sits in but comes alive to
beam when the catch phrases of her husband's songs draw
a laugh.
She wears a blouse of pink satin with masses of carefully
ironed ruffles settled over her broad bosom, and a brown
tweed skirt.

*"But it's oh! oh! in the wintertoim … It's anuvver fing,
you know … Wiv a little red nose … Ahnd very little
clothes … Ahnd the stormy winds do blow-oh-oh … Ahnd
the stormy winds do blow!"*

"They didn't give hurricanes names in those days! They
hadn't had a hurricane in living memory. Nobody knew
what was happening. When the eye came people went
back outdoors. Then it hit again. Well, she was pulling
at her two pickneys, two little girls, to get them into the
old government building. That's the post office now. That
piece of tin roof came sailing on the wind, took her head
off clean as a knife. Abner ran out and pulled in the babes
just ahead of the tidal wave."

"Old Jenk rode his boat right through the main streets of
this town on that tidal wave. When the water dropped he

had to have his boat dragged to the river. Then he went down the river to the ocean."

Mr. Frazier is in his sixties. His skin is pink and white. His hair is white. He wears a white suit. Every evening at sunset he walks his two white, fluffy dogs on the foreshore. "When they were clearing the mud away they found her body but they never found her head."

The regiments stationed here and in Jamaica traditionally go on to actual fighting, if there is actual fighting to go on to. For some time now, there always is.
The Gloucestershires went from here to Korea, where a battalion was massacred down to forty survivors.

•   •   •

Do you believe that we must "deal" with the past?
Remember it, however imperfectly, sift through the bits, have it in mind again, this time as if one *knows* something?
Psychiatrists say so but they're so greedy for provenance. They want everything. To be our all in all.
Then the hour's up and we walk outside into the weather, get into a car, head for the freeway.

You're blessed if you've never been on the road and driving, semi-mindless, and from nowhere been struck to the heart by remorse.
It's a thing the mind does.

In the almighty list of things the mind does, remembering looms large. As immediate as reaching for the cup you just put down.
The subheadings are a list longer than your arm.

The remembering mind fills in the gaps.
In French class when I was asked to translate and I hadn't
studied the lesson my mind would leap at meaning in any-
thing I thought I recognized.
"Since I gave those fools my city they've been fools there."
Mademoiselle would look at me, a blank look of dislike.
"Sometimes the city lifts its roof and looks out just to see
what kind of day it is."
"Sit down, please," Mademoiselle would say coldly and
go on to someone she could count on.

In Belize, young and ignorant as I was I have no idea of
how often my foolishness was covered over by social manners, no one to say "Sit down."
("You only horrified me once, my dear," Alicia said years
later in London. "It was when you came to play tennis
and you were wearing black shorts and a red shirt!")

The remembering mind justifies after the fact.
"I don't understand why every time you talk about that marriage you deprecate yourself for having been there. It was
a very real piece of luck and you took it. It was obviously
a godsend. Why do you think you did something wrong?"

"I really do believe that the only reason to marry somebody is because you love them."
And Dr. Baum laughed, probably to show me it was
laughable.

The remembering mind keeps it real, recognizes error, re-
gains perspective given the new context.
You know that chill when you've identified something at
a distance by sight or sound and it's come nearer to be
something equally understandable but it's something else?
There's a chill, a split second, while the mind makes the shift.
Then it's, I used to be wrong but now I'm right.

I used to think I wanted to be a sophisticate, but now I see it's not in me.

I'll forever be just me again pushing hope and theory in lieu of experience, and backing it up with a little bit of courage and a lot of ignorance. (My grandmother said, "You don't have to be ashamed of having ignorance and lice. You just have to be ashamed of keeping them.")

When Axel got Zaydie (and then others) to bed, it was shattering to me. I hadn't expected to be shattered, not according to the theory of the able sophisticate who is one because she says so.

Axel didn't notice I was feeling it, that he was jubilant at his run of luck.

After all he was only being consistent.

The remembering mind creates a future by remembering that there is one because there always has been. Like a watch that won't work reminds you of time.

I recovered and got on with my own living.

Hope's a floater but a little esprit-de-gumption is as good as credit.

And there was even a relief in it, that love wasn't there and wouldn't be.

Nothing was really changed.

Of course it would have been better to have had that marriage be a permanent possibility with "daisies pied and violets blue"; to have been in love and loved back.

But Axel and I didn't join that statistic.

And once it was clear to me that the way we were was the way we would be, and the six months of grieving for that fact was past (down really deep I was the only one who knew it), then it became not all that much a lost love: more like a theory that fell short.

The Sergeant-Major has begun to sing, *"If you peek in my gah-zee-bo when you are passing by..."*

Joan has had two ducks stolen.
"You *know*, my dear, I'd *never* have eaten them. But *somebody* has stolen them and *eaten* them. It makes me *furious* to think that someone has had the *good* of my two ducks!"

"You'll see a sight that will dee-light the most fahs-tid-ee-us eye!"

Joan's daughter, who is eighteen, has begun to flirt with sweet-faced Richard who is nineteen and, by his own admission, wet behind the ears.

If the Sergeant-Major were singing Brecht he could ask, "Ah, where will we all be a year from today."

Sometimes I feel I live in this world like a tenant.
If I didn't see that a lot of people feel the same I'd think it came from being born a Texas Baptist.
"Just passing through" is a religious term where I came from.
All the Baptists were stopping just long enough to pick up their tickets. Their lives were a perpetual middle and their destinations straight up or straight down.
This "middle" worked them from light to dark, "from can to can't," all the week long with the weather for them or against them.
Back-breaking just begins to describe it. It was face-breaking, hope-breaking. (One year when it looked like my Uncle Peter was going to make a crop after having had to plant three times [the first time a dust storm got it, the

second time a heavy rain packed the seed down] then he
fell into his harrow and messed up his leg so that it took
three operations and every penny he had to set it straight.)
Then on Sundays they'd dress in their best and stand in
some old board building and sing, *"Oh, this is like heaven
to me ... This is like heaven to me ... I've crossed over
Jordan to Canaan's fair land ... And this is like heaven
to me."*
If you think that sounds desirable you weren't there.
And you probably grew up in the city.
I remember it as how to live with heartbreak.

When I got my body back from the Baptists I resisted re-
ligion with rules thereafter. Like an allergy.

"You don't believe in heaven, do you?" Alicia asked, her
voice sad. She knew the answer.
She wasn't going so far as to ask whether I believed in
God; it would have been too devastating.
"No, I don't."
She sighed.
If you don't believe in heaven and hell then you don't get
the simplified up and down.
The pattern is instantly random and the options are more
like something hit the floor and splattered.
It's when you face your own choices that you join the
human "fall."
You come into existence as your own self and there goes
Eden.
And if you decide to not turn into your Mom and Dad,
then whatever your age and however fatuous you are,
what comes next are choices.
For choices you need to have some grasp of the terms.
And the terms won't stand still and let you.

Did you ever go after a cow that didn't want to be caught?
It walks along in an early morning meadow that's slushy
from the weather and you don't even want to be up that
early but that damned cow has to be milked and you take
the rope to slip it over her head and get on a warm jacket
and mud boots if you're lucky and hit the field. That cow
if it glances around at all doesn't seem to notice you all
that much. All it's doing is strolling. And it strolls just as
fast as you walk from the time you've reached its flank. If
you walk faster it strolls faster. If you run it gives a little
spurt and gets well ahead and slows to a stop then starts
strolling again.
The terms stay just that far out in front.
And if you get the rope over and do that morning's milking you haven't gained an inch on this evening's milking
or tomorrow morning's.

"You believe in heaven," I said to Alicia.
"Oh, yes."
"What do you think heaven is like? Do you think you
keep your own body there? Do you keep on being you?"
"Of course I will still be me!"
When I was very young I thought heaven must be an endless meadow where I could ride my horse. In Poland, in
my family, we were taught to ride very young. I was much
younger than my brothers and sisters so they all rode very
well when it was that I must learn. It seemed to me that I
was the only one in the world who did not know how to
ride a horse. And I was frightened of horses. I was terrified. Every day I would be crying when the riding master
would put me onto my horse. My older sister, Heloise,
would laugh.
She said I cried so much because I was a gypsy. She was
terrible to me sometimes when we were children. I was
the only one of the children in my family to be dark like
my father's people. Heloise said that my hair was brown

because I was a gypsy. She said the gypsies had left me on the doorstep and *her* mother and father had taken me in, but I was not their child.

She said ladies and gentlemen do not cry.

And every time I fell off my horse the riding master would put me back on again. He was not sympathetic but he was not cruel. He knew I would learn to ride. He knew that it was nothing to fall off a horse but it was everything to stay off.

Then my mother made Heloise stop saying I was a gypsy, and she told me it was not true.

About that time I learned to stay on the horse.

Then it was the case that I had a talent for riding.

I became the best rider of all my family.

I competed in dressage and jumping and I won many trophies and ribbons.

It made Heloise heartsick that I was so good.

And I loved it.

So, when I was a child I thought heaven would be an endless meadow with no fences where I could ride in any direction and not be stopped."

"When you think of heaven now how do you think of it?"

"I think in heaven we have everything we ever wanted."

We were sitting on the sea wall watching the sunset colors change, feeling the soft freshness of the breeze off the water.

"Alicia," I said, to alleviate her sadness at my fatal declaration, "I *like* living my life. This is like heaven to me."

Coda

I've been thinking today, planning a curry, of the sad little wife of the Major, ex-Indian-Army.

She did not cut her wrists when a very usual sexy female arrived to apply for an American visa and on that visit devoured the little Major as if he were a dressed-out partridge. She did cut her wrists on the lady's *second* visit, when the visa was ready and the woman this time around chose to bed with the fat-assed U.S. Vice Consul. It was having her husband returned to her as rejected goods that undid the Major's wife.

In her happier or at least more felicitous days she taught me to make curry. The last time I saw her (we were to leave the following week) was at an official dance. The Major and his wife were in the Governor's party, which meant they must stand at attention just inside the door while the band, to announce the Governor's arrival, played "God Save the Queen."

That arrival, her wrists taped so neatly it was decorative, and herself with her eyes straight ahead of her, herself standing on parade before a roomful of people, most of whom knew her pathetic story to some degree or another.

They were such dowds.

They could never have anticipated such a *romance* as that. (Perhaps that was exactly what won the lady for the Major. Some people of both sexes like nothing so much as to bestow themselves all gift-wrapped to the most unlikely candidate. And then when they choose, to take it all back again.) The Major short and balding, his wife only one more of those incredibly dressed women once to be found in the multitudes living their lives out in backwater British colonies.

The malice of that woman's choice, the dowdy Major, and the ridiculous pathos of the later-known stories, that the wife had bedded down on the couch to save them all from gossip.

I went home from that dance alone, Axel having many young women to say his goodbyes to.

At the club Saturday nights I could say, "Do you know who the most beautiful woman in the room is?" after having watched him ogle the lot.

"That one?"

"No, that one over there in the far corner. In the white dress."

And he would look, as if hypnotized, to agree that yes she was the most beautiful woman in the room and move to join her company.

I was never a contender.

A letter from Gordon says, "How long ago it seems and I have no nostalgia left for those Belize days. Belize too broken and after Hurricane Hattie it was awful. We were not sorry to get away."

And he says, "Where you lived stood. Lindstrom's house
was totally down and Sir John was laconic and Lady
Agatha mental, I thought, and quite funny and pathetic."
And he says, "Belize, a monumental ruin."

I loved that place and it sometimes seems as if the only
friends in my life were there, perhaps forever true, coming
as I have to be so ambivalent that I must weigh every piece
of cheese pro and con.
Still, if I exaggerate, the place and the people have been
changed.
No one left to contradict or distinguish between the memories I stored even as they happened, knowing I would
want them later; the sadness in that forethought; I loved
it there; a kind of homesickness as if I walked backward.
And the memories of *now*, rising up, that I didn't know
I had.
As when I touched the Major's wife's wrists to say, "Did
you hurt yourself?" she winced so deeply I was struck
silent.
Remembering only then the bit of story I'd heard that
afternoon, why her wrists were bandaged. Wondering,
shocked, how I could have forgotten.
How could I have forgotten?

En Route
(1982)

A simple plan. Get to Guatemala City on a hundred dollars. Non-stop. Take turns sleeping and driving. Cans of tuna, boxes of crackers. Canned milk for the babies. Gallon jugs of water. Diaper pail. Sweaters. Comic books. The baby's mattress fitted over the motor casing at the far back. A folding gate kept her there and opened to the inside. She could be brought in onto the double bed mattress from the inside. The double bed mattress was on top of a plywood platform. Under the platform were all our transportable worldly possessions.

"What are you doing with those boxes?"

"Making boxes."

I sawed through an infinity of cardboard and reassembled it to make boxes for every niche, to fit it all in.

In a small box on the floor in front was what we'd need when somebody started vomiting. Entero-via-forma, Neo-mycina, Kaopectate.

On the shelf made by pulling the double bed mattress as close to the door as it would go, the shelf along the entire far side, where a progressive chaos of all the things

I've mentioned grew, there was also a large empty pot, to be vomited into.

Even madness has its order.

We were as prepared as we could be to begin.

We added ourselves and left.

The metal box of the van was an oven in the northern Mexico desert. Approaching Mexico City. It was the cheapest VW van for the time, a Kombi, with no interior lining of any kind, the metal chilled the interior air and we froze. Beyond Mexico City we drove down into the rain.

Early mornings we stopped in market places, whatever small village or town we were passing. I bought fresh baked bread and fruit. Once a day, in late afternoon, we stopped at a cheap eating place and ate eggs with chili, thin stringy steaks or thin stringy chicken and drank Pepsi.

And arrived at the border to Guatemala to find it closed.

"What does he say?" Patrick asked.

"Whoosh!" the grinning face continued. The border guard raised both arms over his right shoulder and slung downward diagonally across his chest. "Whoosh!"

"Landslide."

Border guards who are decent speak baby talk. The mean ones refuse to and hours go by pointing at dictionaries. Until they are satisfied and want us gone. This one was decent.

"Quando es la frontera possible?"

"Martes."

"Tuesday. He thinks it'll be open Tuesday."

Drive back along what you had hoped to see the last of. The end of Mexico and we're going the wrong way.

A sputtering of light, as loose light bulbs sputter, once, then twice. The beginning of a small miracle. The water on the windows slowed. A curtain opened onto the expanding world. Into that world, faintly at first, growing stronger, the sun began to shine.

"We could have been there," I yelled, in the new quiet of no rain I realized I'd been yelling for days, "tonight," I said more softly.

It was a blessing, despite the disappointment, to stop driving. Enforced rest. Rest without guilt.

I had not known how tired I was, how tired we all were, bringing bags from the van to the small pink hotel on the town's plaza.

Beds and doors to close.

Oh, I'll never die. I'll never die sings in my head like a song, the other words forgotten. I'm slightly delirious arrived in Heaven. I'm happy to be. I'm sitting on a pink chair. Patrick is sitting on a pink chair. We are drinking cold dark beer. We are in sunshine. Wonderful pink. Purple bougainvillea on the far wall and a mean macaw who can't be got near. He bites. Showing us, the woman whose place this is took one finger between the fingers of the other hand and pulled, her face painful. Clean as ballet her hand let loose her hand, and both hands opened, fingers up, palms to hold a bowl, and her face registered amazement at the fact. What can be done, hands and face pantomimed the fact. I would solve it if I could. It is true the bird bites!

How graceful she is. Women in America who are short and dumpy lose their grace for shame. Distress ruins all the rest they might have been. She is charming and good to us. Dispatched the two older girls to the kitchen to help with the tortilla press. A maid, a young woman, her daughter, perhaps, is playing with the babies.

The drying blue and yellow tile floor steams gently. The sunshine is more intense. Soon we must move into the shade of a small orange tree.

I know time has passed because things have changed. The babies are asleep in that room there where the door is open. Through the arch that leads to the street the park shines vivid greens. The two older girls are playing there.

It all has expanded, time is a soft balloon growing.

I know time has passed by the number of beer bottles accumulating on our table. We keep them to be our clock. Empty beer bottles tick off this eternal hour.

Heavenly rest.

"Como gente," Patrick says into the drowsing afternoon that will never go away and leave us.

Like people.

Into this paradise, as particular as the devil into Eden, or does dogma have it that he was always there? Into this blessed moment came Henry.

It's enough to drive you to drink, those people who do infest the heavens of this earth and believe the places are added to by their presence. Those pale blue canvas shoes with crepe rubber soles and "faded blue" denim pants, not faded at all but colored that color. The boyish, knowledgeable look that covers over sins they'll always justify with words and never look in the face.

Well, can any of us bear it, the places in our person that are trashy and spill forth when we least want it.

Of course Henry, walking, covers himself totally over with a surface and swears by it. The kind of person who brags to you if he has contempt for you and doesn't have to question his social manner. And licks your boots when you've got your bluff in on him.

Henry arrived to save us from our own mistake, letting the girls play in the park.

"Oh yes, I've read some of your things," Henry said to Patrick and became more substantial. Became, instead of a concerned person who must correct our misunderstanding, a person who had found another person of like interest. Now we could be told the structure of his life, to see it was interesting.

"I'm a writer myself," Henry lounged back in his pink chair. "No money in it, of course," it sounded like the password into a secret society of two, the two-of-us-men-writers in-the-world, with values like "no money."

"I get my daily bread in the Creative Writing game."

He is a tenured professor, and he has it down, his rap, so well that he can stress the value of "tenured" with a wry look to show his shackles.

"Good money in it?" Patrick asked, his eyes half-closed.

"Oh yes," and for a moment it looked like our new-found acquaintance would display enthusiasm. "Well," he went back to wry, "they pay me the going rate."

He was here on sabbatical, which meant they also paid him for not teaching Creative Writing.

"Twelve rooms for about twenty dollars a month. Food runs a couple of dollars a day."

He had a bargain here.

His twelve room house housed himself and his wife and seven children.

"Would you like to come and have what we laugh-ingly call 'comida'? The children can play together and we can talk."

We would.

Como gente.

Henry's house was a square of rooms all opening into the central courtyard, cobbled and charming with an old stone well that was now only decorative. The courtyard was filled with children and a gray haired woman named Charlotte, who was introduced as "My wife's mother."

The two older children, a boy of nine and a girl who was ten, were from Henry's first marriage. The younger four ranged from seven to two. There was also a baby tucked away somewhere.

"I married the first time for *love*," Henry said bitterly. "I never made *that* mistake again!" And took us through a medieval kitchen, damp and rotting, into a kitchen yard to meet his second wife.

Mrs. Henry was grabbing the sunshine to wash clothes in a tin tub and hang them on a rope to dry.

"This is where the servants stay," Henry said, and laughed to show it was a joke.

Mrs. Henry didn't laugh and didn't stop washing clothes.

There was no question of her joining us. We were more than "como gente" we were "como elegentes," strolling back away from the work.

I slowed, stopped to chat. Mrs. Henry wouldn't look up.

I was interrupting. I had no business there.

I rejoined the two men who were both listening to Henry talk.

He knew so much. He was not over-pleased to see me. He would have chuckled and sent me to the kitchen yard if he had known how.

I sat on a stone step, in the sunshine, and watched the children play, watched the flowers cover over the rotting plaster and let my own exhaustion cover over the sight of that sad ruined woman.

Maybe they're having a fight. When we're fighting it joins all the past fights and feels like all we've ever done is fight. I don't have to like Henry. I want the girls to have a chance to run. I want to laughingly eat comida.

The likelihood of laughter in this place is doubtful.

"Charlotte, have you seen the small tortoise-shell box that should be on my dressing table?" Henry had the clear hard tones of the Boss who has no time for argument.

Charlotte went off obediently to find Henry's misplaced box.

"Here. Try this," Henry handed us each a bit of bark. "Just hold it under your tongue."

Perhaps Henry has redeeming qualities. I looked at
my bit. Patrick looked at his. We obediently put the bits
under our tongues and waited to see what might happen.
I felt my mouth slowly go numb. My tongue went thick.

"You feeling anything?" Patrick asked with a thick,
deadened tongue.

"Interesting, hmmm?" Henry asked. "The Indians
here use it for toothache."

Charlotte returned, carrying a small brown box.

"I didn't *want* the box, Charlotte," Henry's voice was
the voice of a man who deserves better. "I don't *need* the
box. I asked you whether it's where it's supposed to be!"

"Oh, it *was*," Charlotte said, as fervently as if Henry
had just been proven right again. "It was right where you
said it *should* be!"

"Then would you *please* put it back!"

Charlotte left again.

I took the bark out of my mouth when I learned there
was no pleasure in it, as did Patrick. Feeling was slowly
returning.

Henry flourished two glasses and poured into one of
them from the green bottle. Red wine.

He reached past me to give the glass to Patrick.

"I find this wine is too harsh for women," he explained, bobbing his head in agreement with himself.

I could tell than no less harsh wine would be forthcoming. You silly, drab piece of goods! I'm not caught in
your reality! I *mean* to have a glass of that predictably
lousy wine!

"I've been married to a writer for four years now," I
said firmly. "I can drink almost anything."

It was a joy to see Henry be inconvenienced. The second glass which he had filled for himself must be handed
to me. He must put the bottle down to have both hands to
help him rise. He played the part of a cripple. Every step

hurt. Back to the glasses. I thought he well might drop one just to prove how far I had gone wrong. He walked the long way back. And he must sit down. And he must fill the third glass. And now he must smile, being the host who had proved to be a better host than anyone deserved. He smiled. When Patrick raised his glass to me so, unexpectedly, did Henry.

My beloved Patrick is a man who delighted me from my first sight of him. Diffident and quiet he throws a look as bright as color through crystal. We had been married then for four years and his conversation could still catch my imagination and sling it distances. Any other man was negligible in my eyes.

Henry, bad at his best, was a posturing robot.

Enough bad wine on an empty stomach and rhapsodies. Rhapsody. Darling Patrick.

My life has been blessed by a various man.

I smiled at him and he smiled back.

"My star pupil!" Henry interrupted his own monologue to introduce Chuck, another of his endless menage. Chuck, plump and pimply, had come through a far door, and here he was, to join us.

There was no question of Henry going for another glass.

"He'll make a first-rate writer!" The implication was that Henry was molding a masterpiece in this pathetic creature.

Chuck preened, given his prospects. All his pudgy stuff was held quiescent willingly, to be punched into shape.

Bottle number two of the wine, that was no harsher than I was accustomed to, materialized, and was drunk without Chuck being offered any by the man who meant to mold him. Some molding had obviously already gone down. Henry must have often sat at the table drinking

to his heart's content on this wine that was too harsh for
women, children, and Chuck.

Our party of three was becoming jolly.

Chuck's consolation is that he can go for more.

Before he could be allowed out of the house he must remember a certain structure of marks and letters that should be on the label.

"If it's the good stuff!" Henry insisted, and pointed them out. "If those marks aren't on the label don't let them sell it to you. He'll try to tell you it's the same but it's not. You tell him to bring more from the back room."

Henry spoke as if Chuck spoke Spanish. It had come out in earlier conversation that Chuck spoke no Spanish and an uninspired English.

"He'll know you're onto him! He'll know what's up!"

Thus armed Chuck is set to sally forth.

My head is spinning. Comida is a long time coming.

"I'll go with you." And I stand.

Good idea. I wasn't in a ridiculous state but I could do with a walk.

"Why don't you take the empty bottle?" and Chuck grabbed at it like any item deserves to be grabbed that can save a life.

"You don't need that!" Henry frowned. "You should be working on your Spanish!"

"*I* need it, Henry." It seems that it is allowable to Henry for me to nurture my ignorance.

Chuck, the bottle, and I walked out onto the street that loomed large after the strictures of the patio.

Look that household over. Seven kids from one to ten. Second wife living up to the strictures of lacklove. Charlotte for an occasional snack and Chuck for God knows what.

In the buzz got from sharing two seventy-five cent bottles of wine on an almost empty stomach did I worry that my fine Patrick had a recognizable gleam in his eye, was in the beginnings of one of his notorious drunken bits of behavior and would, in all likelihood, direct it toward ghastly Henry?

I did not.

Every move Henry made defined him as deserving another treatment than his defaulted household had given him.

"Why does your husband call him Hank?" Chuck asked. "Henry doesn't like to be called Hank. He doesn't let anyone call him Hank."

"Say that, Chuck, and you've said it all."

"What?"

"I said 'you said it,' Chuck."

"What?"

Chuck made no effort to improve his Spanish, shoved the empty bottle at the man on sight. That was good enough for the wine merchant. He searched the shelves, got one bottle, looked at Chuck who held up two fingers, got another, went for a bag, looked up, surprised, when Chuck snatched the bottles from his hands. He stood, puzzled, while Chuck, prepared to kill for quality and his master's voice earnestly examined the labels. The marks were there. Chuck treated it as a personal coup.

Henry had reintroduced his original theme. Prestige in the outback nations.

"Only the Indians let their girls go into the street without a servant," he said with the righteousness of a naturally superior person who had lucked out, come a few thousand miles south and found the nation of naturally inferior persons. Now all he needed to do was maintain the status quo.

It suited him, this poverty he was no part of. Born to be free and own it. All of it.

"When I walk with Maria she doesn't allow me to walk in the street," Henry's oldest daughter made a bid for her father's attention. "When someone comes toward

us on the sidewalk and there's not enough room she won't
let *me* step off. *They* have to step off."

"It's a question of position," Henry approved.

"Oh, yes, indeed," Patrick sang without a tune, and turned his first corner in the afternoon and was swacked enough to burst into his brand-new pseudo old-time-ditty. "They learn their dirty little lessons at their jolly daddy's knee."

"A necessary lesson!" Henry said pompously. "One of the *necessary* lessons!"

"Oh yes!" Patrick never had a voice to be listened to over-much. Not a singing voice. "Necessary...authoritary...dirty daddy's...knee...eee...eee!"

Pause, while the gentleman who knows better decides to take no notice.

"Perhaps I should see to the meal," Henry said, rising to do so. His wisest move of the day.

"Too late," Patrick sang. "Too-oo late! All my fondest hopes are dead... Three little words. Those words were ne-eh-eh-ehver said!"

Henry had gone to confer with his wife. It seemed there was no coffee in the house and she must go for some.

He came back into the dining room where we were sitting with our glasses of wine and sat again at the head of the table. Mrs. Henry followed after and hung at Henry's shoulder, her eyes on him, as intent as if he were the cliff she hung from.

This was the first long look we had of her. In contrast to Henry's unlikeable prime she was withered and tired beyond rest. She could have been, if not his mother, his aunt. An old maid aunt kept by his charity, a permanent plea for... mercy?... consideration... in her eyes. There was a sense to her of sore edges, lines of pink where she had been rubbed so raw at the edges of her eyelids, the tips of her thin fingers that moved in a perpetual nervous little rub. She breathed through her mouth and where her lips were slack a pink line showed.

Henry was speaking to us as if she were not there.

"You can't send a servant for coffee. They'll give them the poorest kind of bean."

He meant to buy just enough coffee for one pot. He stipulated that it be green.

She's going to have to roast it and grind it and make it. That puts food back awhile. Patrick's condition, gauged with a wifely eye... food would help. Patrick looked up at me and winked and grinned to show he knew what and where and when.

"She can't keep servants. She doesn't treat them with authority so they lose respect for her and leave."

Imagine that poor ruin of a woman showing authority. It would be good for her if she could. It would take as much as hell freezing over. Just that much of a shift.

"You know we've been here a *long* time," I said to Henry. "We could just as easily go back to the hotel and see you tomorrow."

By tomorrow she might have dealt with the coffee. Or they could come to the pink hotel and we could have something there without her having to cook it.

Why had we stayed so long in this molasses that by now was up to my neck.

"I know she's slow but she only has one servant to help her," Henry chided me. Mrs. Henry looked at me with a clear flash of anger. I was giving Henry more justification to do her down.

OK I'll stay. We'll all stay. The children are playing happily at last. It would be great to eat something well-cooked.

In my heart of hearts I *know* that woman is not a good cook.

OK.

Another glass of wine.

Patrick could have backed me up and we'd be on our way out now. Drinking wine all afternoon does away with scruples.

"Charlotte!"

Henry had reached into his pockets and found no money there.

"I need some money for coffee."

She's running. She runs from her room to answer his call. She runs back to her room for her purse. She returns, running, to the table digging into her purse as she comes. She arrives holding a crumpled mass of notes toward Henry.

This household is an insane household. Were they all this crazy before they met each other? Henry certainly owns the motor but does that mean he's trained them to be his kind of insane? Did he find them standing on a corner, waiting for a boss?

Are we fascinated also? It's true that Patrick can't keep his eyes off the proceedings. What's going on in his head would make a book. This afternoon stretches out like rubber. Is it exhaustion or fascination that keeps us here in this long stretch caught into Henry's world, watching him cook the afternoon in his pot, stir the ingredients with his ladle.

He fastidiously lifted a ten-peso note out of the pile offered to him by Charlotte and handed it to her daughter.

She took it, girded up her courage and left the table, left the patio through the door onto the street.

No chance for me to say a word to her. What could I have said that might have made sense? Take the money and run. When you're through that door notice it. You're out. You've escaped.

People protect themselves from the messages they don't want to hear. They don't hear, won't hear what makes them think about what they can't bear to think about. Struggling makes it hurt more. Like quicksand. One of my bits from childhood's accumulation of useless but glamorous esoteric knowledge: if you struggle in quicksand you sink faster.

Maybe the two of us can get the kids into the van tomorrow and have a picnic. Maybe I can drive her to the nearest airport and give her the money and say fly away.

Mrs. Henry, it's probable, never leaves the house for pleasure. Mrs. Henry only goes out to do Henry's errands.

Henry reached from where he sat to a shelf behind him and lifted a blue bound pamphlet from a stack of others just like it.

"I published this last year in the East Coast Review."

He has two hundred copies made of his eight pages. Had them bound to be a publication. Him by him.

He wrote on the first page.

To Patrick Dougherty, At The End Of The Road…
Henry.

"This *is* where the Pan American Highway ends, you know," he explained. "It doesn't pick up again until much farther down."

Henry's wife returned. She came back through the dining room to give the change to Henry and continued on her way to the kitchen with a small paper bag of coffee.

"Where's the rest?" Henry hissed. She froze in place. She turned. She returned to the table.

"That's all he gave me. That's all the change he gave me."

"I gave you *twenty pesos!* Where is the other ten peso note?"

Is this a routine they need spectators for? Henry must get an extra charge out of the additional humiliation his cohorts go through with an audience.

If we were to jump up screaming, clobber Henry, would he suddenly smile, would all of them chuckle and Henry turn into a show-biz personality before our eyes and point to the wall behind him and say "Smile, you're on Candid Camera!"

No.

Never in this world.

"You gave her ten pesos, Henry," I said.

"I must have left it on the counter," Mrs. Henry was believing him. Charlotte was keeping mum.

"I'll go back," and she turned to leave, to go back to the coffee shop for ten pesos invented into the air by her husband.

"It wouldn't be there now! You don't think it will still be there! Somebody else has it by now!"

Mrs. Henry stood, slumped and frozen in place. Can't go backward. Can't go forward. Hopeless.

"You only gave her ten pesos, Henry."

"Get on with the meal!" Henry snapped. It makes a man snappish to bear such a burden, to be surrounded by fools who must be told every little thing.

"Can I help you?" I asked.

She shook her head no.

Patrick stood. Went to a far wall for a chair. Put it between the two of us.

"Sit down."

"She has things to do if we're ever going to eat!"

"Let her do them here. A little bit of fun does the workers good, Hank."

"Sit down," Henry hissed at his wife, furious. "For Christ's sake stop making such a scene!"

Told what to do she did it. Sat down. Not much bit of fun in it. She sat at the table, as oppressed as if she had gone to the kitchen. She poured out a little pile of the coffee beans and began to peel them.

Peel the beans?

"What are you doing?" I asked. God, everything I said to her took on Cosmic proportion. Can I help you and what are you doing rang with portent.

"The quality of the coffee is much improved when the peel isn't included in the roasting and the grinding."

"You did give her *ten* pesos, Henry," I grabbed the chance to get it across, now that we were conversing.

"So since we're here with the best coffee in the world it would be foolish not to have it."

I turned to Mrs. Henry.

"Henry did only give you ten pesos. He gave you the ten peso note he borrowed from your mother."

Mrs. Henry would not look up. She only saw the pile of coffee she was peeling with her bitten fingers.

"OK then," I took a handful of the coffee beans for me to peel. "In fact!" I took the rest, laid out a small pile in front of Patrick, Chuck, Henry, the oldest daughter.

We all peeled coffee beans.

Now Mrs. Henry had only to roast the coffee, grind the coffee, make the coffee, and we would have coffee.

Comida was beans and tortillas, wilted lettuce and a slice of tomato, and coffee. The coffee was terrible. The comida was not laughable.

"This is a little something I gave my freshmen class last year. You might find it interesting."

PRINCIPLES OF ENJAMBMENT: ILLUSTRATIONS

"You use enjambment?" Henry asked Patrick, off-handed, shop-talk among men who knew these distinctions.

"I do enjamb, Hank," Patrick said seriously.

We've got to get out of here. The meal and bad coffee off-set the wine and I found myself with no desire to see Henry, unsalvageable, no one home, natural monster, confronted by Patrick, shape changer extraordinaire, given the inclination and a taste of the old potion.

"Let's go home," I poked Patrick on the arm.

"Let's go to the cantina," he answered.

"OK. Let's go to the cantina."

Anyplace out of here is a beginning.

"Have a look at what Henry does," he passed over the two pages of enjambment,

> It quickened next a joyful Ape, and so
> Gamesome it was, that it might freely goe
> From tent to tent, and with the children play.

While I read, Henry went to where the children played and there were the sounds of children being whipped.

He returned.

"The children have torn up the maid's supper. The tortillas that were left were for her. They tore them up to play house with and now she'll have to go without supper. I've punished my two oldest children for not supervising the young ones better."

He crossed his arms and waited. The ball was in our court. He expected us, in all decency, to punish our children also.

Patrick rose, went into the patio. He fumbled in his pocket for a couple of almost valueless coins and handed them to the maid. "Tortillas," he told her. He patted whatever children were nearby on their heads and returned.

"Hank, let's get this show on the road. Let's go to the cantina."

Before we left Henry made his final addition to Patrick's growing pile of Henry's claim to fame, a thirty-one page poem in manuscript. In a hard-cover folder. Henry described it. A romantic theme. Ballad form. A personal, innovative method.

Our being in town for a few days meant that there was time enough for Patrick to give Henry's long poem his careful attention and there was time enough for the two of them to talk it over.

Patrick turned a few of the pages in quietly increasing despair.

"Lots of enjambment in there, Hank."

Henry smiled, then frowned.

I stopped at the hotel to see the children settled. Told the maid where I would be, three doors down, at the cantina on the corner.

Walking alone along a dark night street in Mexico lifts the spirits.

Moments like this thread through all our lives in a loose mesh, join to make a size we join, in moments like this.

The cantina was where Hank had said it would be. The furnishings were a few wooden tables that didn't match and a variety of rough wooden chairs. The décor was paper flowers put there long ago and never reconsidered, faded to dirty gray. On the tables glass jars printed with religious images held small candles.

Where Patrick, Henry, and Chuck sat the glass jar had a decal of the Virgin Mary holding her infant. The candle had burned half way down her body, the flame was bright in her belly.

Chuck was nervous, tried to see in every direction. He had had bad experiences in Mexican bars.

"… he just picked up a beer bottle and broke it on the bar…"

Patrick also was looking around. Patrick's face was gleeful. Patrick was looking for the action.

Patrick attracts whatever action is going.

In Vera Cruz the first summer after we were married he would go to the Plaza at night while I stayed home with the children.

The next day there would always be stories. He had gone around through restaurants with an armless beggar. Patrick had somehow come by a violin and he fiddled and passed the hat while the beggar danced.

You should know that Patrick doesn't lie.

Sometimes, it's true, alcohol does obscure degree. That is, I'm sure he did play fiddle but when he also insisted that he played it beautifully, that all his childhood lessons bore fruit in one grand musical coup, I'm inclined to doubt it.

After only a few days in Vera Cruz he could point as we drove past to the third floor of a decaying building and say "That's where the Japanese man with the two children lives." And I could look at the building where that gentleman had taken Patrick, worried for him, and fed him soup. There had been two small children there who must be left alone while their father worked at his job.

"Their mother is dead," Patrick told me, returning home in the early morning. "He came home one night and she was dead on the floor."

Another night the first mournful and hopeless thing he had to say was, "I've lost the car."

"You *lost* the car?"

"I lost the car. It isn't anywhere."

"You just forgot where you parked it. We'll go out after breakfast and look for it."

"They stole it. Somebody stole my car."

"We'll find it. Get in bed. Go to sleep."

"That's it is it! Just 'go to bed' 'go to sleep.' That's the best you can do when somebody steals my car!"

"We'll find it, Patrick. It's too dark to go look for it now. When it's light we'll go find it!"

He grumbled himself to sleep. He was hurt. I laid awake. A woman who couldn't sympathize with a man who's lost his car.

The car was parked in the block near the Plaza that had a street light. Patrick wanted to say "They brought it back" but knew better.

Henry, it seems, *could* distinguish when forced between usual women and other women. Usual women, in his experience of it, were terrorized, stayed decently at home, were wives like his own. Any woman not of his marriageable category must be the *other*. The *other* must be all else. The *other* was "such stuff as dreams are made of."

I had become glamorous in Hank's eyes.

The way a man with a maid is an endless source of wonder. What he manifests of himself, drawn forth from heartfelt depths, can confuse and confound anyone who has only seen him in his mundane guise, without the glow of the glamoured mind that lights a light behind the eyes and makes the body graceful. Everyone feels improved in that moment, remembers their daily mundane person as the shaded part of this, their better self. And so it was with Henry.

He caused a lugubrious rendering of "Quando Me Tiquieros" to be played on the jukebox and knew all the words, and sang them in my ear.

"I like Rancheros, myself," I said tartly.

Hank was momentarily crushed. Was this rejection?

He bought a flower from the barman and laid it alongside my glass of beer.

Chuck scuttered his chair sideways, against mine, he would have pushed through me if I had been less substantial.

His fears had been realized.

The space he cleared at the table was crashed against by the drunk who had crossed the room, intent on our little group.

Standing stopped he rolled on his two feet as if the floor were in heavy seas.

He looked at Chick, at me, at Henry, his lip snarled and ugly.

"Gringos!" He spat on the floor.

Chuck, almost in my lap, began to whisper toward me, his eyes caught and glued to the borracho's face.

"He means trouble! He's going to cause trouble!"

The borracho sneered around the table until he came to Patrick.

There is a vast understanding among drunks. Like dogs and small children they recognize one another across all barriers. They stare, their faces tightening to look. All else fades into the background.

Patrick waved one arm in a splendid gesture.

"Y pues!" he said, almost his total score of Spanish, to his newest long-lost friend.

"Y pues?" the standing drunk asked.

"Y pues!" the seated drunk insisted.

The Mexican reached to the next table and scraped a chair across the intervening floor to put it in the space so recently vacated by Chuck, who sat shivering and terrified by his new neighbor.

They made a charming picture those two, Patrick and the Mexican. The Mexican's arm was laid over Patrick's shoulders as if it were an ornament and he talked, his face screwed into a villainous expression, his mouth spitting. Their faces were a scant inch apart. At intervals the Mexican would wave his free arm at the other three at the table and glare and Patrick would also look at us, his face angelic and delighted, relieved at last of listening to Henry. A friend at last. Whenever the man would stop as if he asked a question Patrick would say "Y pues" and bob his head sympathetically and the Mexican would continue.

Whispered hissing came in both my ears. Chuck on one side. Henry on the other side. An ear apiece.

"... he just picked up a beer bottle and broke it on the bar..."

"Chuck hadn't done *anything!* He was just standing there."

"Right for my face."

"They grabbed him. Four men couldn't hold him!"

"Right for my face!"

"One minute they're smiling."

The borracho stood. His chair fell at his back, crashed to the floor. Chuck and Henry flinched, ready to go under the table.

It was true the standing, weaving Mexican was glaring at them with a venomous intent that stopped short of murder but no one could understand why. He leaned toward them, slowly, keeping his balance, leaning forward more and more until he must hold himself up by putting his hands on the tabletop.

They were transfixed.

Both faces registered horror Hollywood would have paid for. They waited for terrible death.

"Gringos!" he accused them, within inches of their frozen faces.

He spewed them with spit, saying it. His lips and face were twisted with disgust and hatred for them, the enemy. How could he not know them? He began to straighten up, his eyes still on theirs. It took an eternity.

When he was upright he glanced briefly at me. I was uninteresting.

He looked at Patrick. His face melted with tender regard. He lifted his right hand in a soft flourish of farewell, a gesture as pure as an entire ballet. He turned and left, a shambling creature.

Chuck pulled his chair back into place.

"Why did he like *you* so much?" Chuck asked Patrick, jealously. It was a burden to him that the Mexican nation went for his throat on sight.

"He certainly did," Henry agreed. "A kindred soul perhaps."

He meant to decimate what had just happened back into considered opinion and understanding.

Patrick leered at the two who could so quickly resume their roles.

"If you don't know, why ask?"

"Well, I'm for bed."

I felt no pity for Henry's anxiety at being left responsible for Patrick. Said goodnight around the table. Gave Patrick a kiss. Walked three doors down the street to the hotel. Said goodnight to the Indian girl who had stayed with the children. Gave her some money. Checked the sleeping children. Went to bed.

"He *threw* me out of his house!" the wail of a grossly misunderstood man. "He told me, 'Leave!' He said, 'Go home, Patrick Dougherty!'"

The room was dark with a seepage of light through the door. Patrick semi-sprawled on the floor where he had fallen in a long lunge, coming home. At intervals he would try to stand but the flesh was weak.

"*I* said," Patrick drew himself into as dignified a position as was available to him, "*I* said, 'You understand this means the next time we meet I will have to kill you!' And *he* said," he gave up all hope for dignity, laid flat on the floor and giggled, "*he* said, 'Then I must do my best to avoid seeing you!'"

We would not, after all, wait until Tuesday. We would drive to the other coast, the Pacific coast, downhill to sea level, and cross the border to negotiable roads on the train.

It was very possible we might return to the border here on Tuesday and find that more landslides had happened to cut the road off. We would depend on the train.

"What that son-of-a-bitch has on Charlotte is when she got pregnant the man proposed and she turned him down and he went off to war and got killed. Henry says it's Charlotte's fault that he's married to a bastard! Henry's bit is he asks Charlotte why she said no. And Charlotte tries to say what she thinks she remembers was the case!"

Patrick decently laid the manuscript to one side and ripped through the two pages of enjambment and the blue photocopied poem, "At least I don't have to read this shit!" He threw the pieces in the wastebasket.

And I started to laugh.

"I looked at Charlotte and Chuck and Henry's wife waiting to be told it was alright to go to bed and all I could think of to say was 'Hank, enjambment is shit!' That's when he threw me out."

The packing done we went into the patio. One last cup of coffee.

"I said, 'Hank, this town isn't big enough for the two of us!' And he said, 'Well, I was here first!'"

Chuck, perspiring, came through the double doors.

"I'll get Henry's manuscript," Patrick said, left the table.

"I've never *seen* Henry so upset," Chuck said.

"Would you like some coffee? Why don't you sit down."

"Oh, no!" Chuck backed away. He would be asked when he returned to give an exact accounting of all that had happened. Hank would be waiting and suspicious. Hank would know if Chuck had fudged.

Patrick came back, handed into Chuck's hand the hard-cover folder containing Hank's thirty-one page poem (romantic theme, ballad form, innovative mode).

Chuck, being free to go, did. Relieved.

And returned.

Patrick had gone to collect bags. I had begun to collect children.

"Henry wants the examples of enjambment." Chuck's voice was firmer, righteous. Henry spoke through him, remote control.

"Patrick tore them up," I said, smiling.

"He tore them up?"

"He tore them up," I said, quite friendly. "It was just

a mimeographed sheet, Chuck."

"It was the *only* copy he had with him!" Chuck's face was returned to its normally anxious pattern. "He's *really* going to be *mad!*"

And again Chuck left.

Beer and mariachis and pink chairs. A day's rest and re-creation. A day jeweled in sunshine. A day flawed by Hank.

Driving downhill to sea level from the heights of San Cristobal the rain began again. And the steam of sea level heat.

The diapers smelled more when it was hot. And the spills of milk turned sour, that smell smelled more.

This is us and our world. This is us and all the goods with us. We mean to get "there."

Guatemala, 1960/61

Interview:

Bobbie Louise Hawkins with Barbara Henning

(2011)

When I was at the Naropa Summer Writing Program in June 2011, I picked up a copy of Bobbie Louise Hawkins' novel, *One Small Saga*, and read it that same night. It is beautifully written prose with poetic disjunction and rhythm, the story of a young artist on a journey to Belize with her new husband. In the months that followed, I conducted an extensive interview with Bobbie about her writing life. Below is an excerpt from that interview re-edited for the purposes of this book. The entire interview is available at belladonnaseries.org; other sections are included in Bobbie's *Fifteen Poems* (Arif Press, 1974; Belladonna, 2012) and in her *Selected Prose* (Blazevox, 2012).

— *Barbara Henning, 2020*

•   •   •

BARBARA: In your book, *One Small Saga*, the narrator, Jessie, seems to be in a fix. She doesn't have enough money to continue art school and then Axel asks her to marry him.

BOBBIE: I didn't have the money to go to college, and not having the money was the truth of the time, but that wasn't why I went with him. I went with him because it was an adventure. There I am, living with my parents in a two bedroom little house in Albuquerque, and here is this Danish architect from Africa and England, saying that he'd like to marry me and take me out of the country. With Olaf, I felt that I was in a place I already knew. I felt less exiled in that circumstance than I did living in a bedroom in my mother's house. When I got on the ship with Olaf and we set off to Europe, it was like now I was in my life.

BARBARA: When I read the book, I wasn't thinking about it being you. I thought she was a character in a novel, perhaps autobiographical, but fiction, too.

BOBBIE: Robert Duncan once said there is no such thing as fiction. And that makes more sense than almost anything. And when at one point I started looking back through my stories, I thought, I have almost never written a fictional line in my life. Your mind gets on something and you just meander along with it. I don't think that's fiction. It's all autobiography.

BARBARA: Wasn't that what Duncan was talking about in his essay, "The Truth and Life of Myth," that experience and imagination are one. And once you start telling any story, you jump into some fictional realm.

BOBBIE: And you give yourself the allowance to elaborate. The other thing Robert Duncan was very involved in was "persona" so that he would have a poem and he would in effect have the "persona" from which the poem occurred. You look back at different things really bright people have said, and you register how little of it has been followed through on by other writers. But I did lend some of my students this notion of persona as a place to stand and write from. The thing about teaching is that people are going to have to end up doing all of it, just like you did, but they will never get their hands on all of it, like you never did. And what you do—if you're going to stay with any kind of energy at all or any kind of validity—you go with whatever sparks in that moment. And it might be that that moment's spark is the only time that it ever occurs in your life. Just that quick little uptake and then you go past it.

BARBARA: Bobbie, did you write *One Small Saga* while you were experiencing it?

BOBBIE: I don't even remember because an awful lot of

BOBBIE: I don't even remember because an awful lot of 151 my writing is cardboard box writing. I'll choose a bit and I'll do a bit and it's like early on you think you've got these options particularly if you have travelled much. You think, yes, I'll write my London novel. I'll write my British Honduras novel, you know. You start writing about those places and you use up the good material and then you register that if you mean to write a whole novel, this material is going to be like seasoning sprinkled through it and now you are stuck with the tedious part—

BARBARA: Putting it together. You wrote it in small pieces?

BOBBIE: Yes. And then the whole middle. I'd think some more about it. Little tiny lines would come across, some better than others, than some not. So at some point when Allan Kornblum was doing Toothpaste Press [which became Coffee House Press in 1984, the year of *One Small Saga*'s publication], he asked me if I had a book because he wanted to put my name into a grant proposal he was writing. As I tell my students, anytime someone asks you if you are working on a book, the only answer is, yes. And then you go find a book. And I said yes, and then I started pulling this stuff out and putting the stuff that went together in chunks and having a look at it and then sort of lining them up to see where I could fill in.

What I'm really short on is transitions. Fielding Dawson was a brilliant transitional guy. Did you ever read him?

BARBARA: Yes, I teach some of his stories in my classes.

BOBBIE: He wrote an extraordinary book called *The Mandalay Dream*. He was capable of creating an incredible ambiance with the transitional shifts he wrote, and I always envied him for it. My inclination is to give the gist of something and then fade to black and then come up with the next gist of something.

BARBARA: There's all that white space. You dip into a life, and the emotion is intensified by line and language.

BOBBIE: Something happened that I never—I still don't get it—something happened in the shaping of *One Small Saga*. I don't have it to look at. Did I start all the lines from the margin?

BARBARA: Yes, even when you wrote a long paragraph, it was more like a line. So it is written like a poem. It's interesting the way you segue from one point of view to another. Easier to do with lines, I think. Right off, we read differently, expecting an unusual style and form, a prose narrative in lines with gaps.

BOBBIE: I didn't even think about using poetic breaks and lines and stuff. That wasn't the approach. I wasn't finding a shaping theory. It was more like this line isn't working. What can I do? Virginia Woolf said technique is finding the specific form and tone for the individual piece that lets you say everything.

I don't know why that book required that, but it is like that. I kept working on it and working on it and finally that was the format that somehow felt comfortable. And I thought when I was doing it, this works really great. I'm going to do this forever and then as soon as I had finished it, I lost all interest in using that form. I think an awful lot of the blockage you experience when you are writing something has to do with you not yet getting the message from the piece itself, that it has a shape it wants. And when that message gets through, suddenly everything becomes very much simpler.

BARBARA: Remember in the novel, when Jesse meets Axel's sister, she feels utterly in a different world?

BOBBIE: Axel's sister was a different kettle of fish. Axel's sisters, both of them, were ghastly women who weren't very much liked by their parents. They were both bossy and problematic. Birte felt that I didn't appreciate the up-swing in my social position. Olaf's father was a personal friend of the King of Denmark who would drop in for tea. After the Nazis moved into Denmark during the war, Olaf's father was one of the first persons to be put in jail as a potential problem maker. He was a very gentle and nice man, with real status in Denmark as a serious person, and those things about him were just great.

We were on this boat, the *Gripsholm*, going to Europe and because we bought the cheapest tickets, at mealtimes you had a table that was your table with those persons who sat there and here was this one man who was English, like a taxi driver or something, but he was Scandinavian. All of these people were going to Scandinavia as the first Christmas boat that year. This guy was that kind of English cockney thing. He was charming and he was witty and funny and there is Birte sitting there like a great lump. And she really felt obliged to tell me that in Denmark, of course, we would never be associated with a person of his social standing. She was an awful snob.

And the other thing was that Olaf was adopted. Olaf was the son of his mother's first marriage. His mother was an opera singer in Norway, and she had this first marriage and when that marriage ended, she met Mr. Hoeck and they married and he adopted Olaf.

When Olaf and I arrived in Sweden, the night before we were due to arrive in Copenhagen, a lot of Danish newsmen came aboard. They wanted to play up this romance between Olaf and me. So they were talking to us and taking pictures and we were on the front page of two or three newspapers the next day. They were giving Olaf all of this attention and Birte was furious. She was the real daughter and he was only... Every time that woman had room to be bad-hearted, she did it. And she did it all for the sense of her superiority. Well, you have seen people like that.

I got on beautifully with the mother and father. They really liked me. They gave us a large dinner party at their home and everyone was decorating the tree. I grew up an only child. My mother had me when she was seventeen. She would be working as a waitress and that meant she worked these different odd hours. I'd be getting up in the morning and making my breakfast, like cereal or something, dressing myself and going off to school, being at school and coming back and being by myself. As an only child, I really put in a lot of time without anybody else around except for books, and I really believed that the world I read in books existed out there and that there were people who spoke to each other in this ongoing and rational fashion. And that was where I wanted to be.

BARBARA: Before you met Olaf, you were an actor, weren't you?

BOBBIE: When I was about sixteen I got into a repertory company in Albuquerque that was intending to make radio soap operas. I was on a city bus in Albuquerque going east on Central and I saw this building with "Art Center" written across the front in neon. Because I thought of myself as possibly being some sort of artist, I got off the bus and went across the street to see what was going on. I found myself in this building with sound proofing on the walls, with all kinds of microphones, and two major studios, each studio with an engineering room. It was a professional set up. I was shown around, and I asked if I could audition, they said yes. That was a break. I got a lot of training in that situation, and they liked what I did. I was the youngest member of the group, I was sixteen, and there was a lot there for me to learn. I was skipping a lot of school and anytime I could get away, I would go straight there and work on phonetics, for example, which helped me get rid of a Texas accent. I didn't want a Texas accent. I wanted to be an elegant person living in a book.

BARBARA: What books were you reading?

BOBBIE: Oh, honey, anything I could put my hands on. It wasn't as if I had anything like an education. We moved every three months, eight months, so I never finished a year in the same school.

BARBARA: Did your mother take you to the library?

BOBBIE: Oh, no. My mother read magazines. She was enamored of gothic horror so the magazines that were in the house were *Amazing Stories*, *Astounding Stories*, all of these vampire and werewolf stories. When I was six, they brought out a double billing of *Frankenstein* and *Dracula*. My mother who was hardly more than a child herself, longed to go to that. She was worried about taking me with her, that it might be harmful for a six year old to see these two monster movies. But she took me.

BARBARA: I remember seeing those type of movies when I was about that age, too.

BOBBIE: So what I read was a lot of gothic horror stuff. When I was about ten, there was a great American sci-fi renaissance. Suddenly really good writers were writing science fiction, also a lot of bad writers, but these gothic magazines became "Amazing and Science Fiction Stories." They were what was there to read. At different times, I started going to libraries by myself and librarians would become interested in me. So that they would recommend books like all the Oz books. My reading was completely random. I read a lot of comic books. If you read a lot, it almost doesn't matter what you read, your taste is going to improve. The mind rejects boredom. The mind notices when it gets a higher return. When somebody tells beginning writers to just keep on writing, what is hoped for is that by writing an excessive amount they are automatically going to improve.

When I was living in England, in London, there was a library between where I was living and the underground [station]. Since I had that regular walk—I thought I'm going to be here a long time—I just started with the As. It didn't matter if I heard of them or not—I'd just pull a book down and take a taste, looking for something that caught me, and I went through a lot of books, most that I don't remember all that well. And yes, almost all my writing is autobiography because it is almost all the outcome of conjecture. I start thinking about something and it gets hooked in my head. Do you want to hear a good line? Ben Jonson—I came across it a couple of days ago. "A horse that can count to ten is an exceptional horse. It is not an exceptional mathematician." Isn't that great?

BARBARA: It's wonderful.

BOBBIE: I love lines like that. People come up with great lines. With *One Small Saga*, I'd be thinking about something, write a piece down, maybe a paragraph, maybe a page, maybe two pages, and maybe later, I'll think, oh do

that again, do another, and they don't work, but I chuck
them in the box, you know.

BARBARA: It reminds me of Marguerite Duras' book, *The Lover*. Both about young love, both understated but with poetic intensity. Both your book and her book are poetic-fictional-memoir.

BOBBIE: I love that book, and you had earlier mentioned love as a problem in *One Small Saga*. Well, dear, love is always a problem. It doesn't matter if it is in a book or—love isn't at all what it pretends to be. It is essentially a form of self-hypnosis, an obsession. If you watch a cat in heat, you know much more about love than if you read a romance novel. I mean they look so luxurious and lovely and they are stretching and feeling great about themselves. It is wonderful to stretch and feel great about yourself. And then when the person you have manufactured this feeling with or had this feeling with, when they go away, it's like they take it with them. And suddenly you don't even feel the size you were before you met the person. You feel less than that, you feel shrunken. Did you ever read Colette?

BARBARA: Long ago. I haven't in many years.

BOBBIE: There is one point when she reached fifty or sixty, and she wrote a letter to men, and in it she said that obviously at this point she was past the point of romance. Then she began to mention what it was that she would miss, and one of the things she missed was exactly what it is you are saying you hate. What she missed was the complication, the ability to feel disaster, the ability to have your feelings be right out there, extra to your thought process. The big drag is the implication that these things are forever. If we could just get rid of forever. I mean what if

they issued marriage certificates or contracts of relation-
ships or something that said, "I'll give this six months."
"This looks like two weeks to me." You know, it would
really help. As it is, here you are and this is forever. And
as soon as it is not forever, you think, you made a mistake. And you didn't make a mistake. You just got on to
something with a shorter shelf life than you had thought.

You know, thinking about that Marguerite Duras book,
she's writing about the young girl. But how old was she
when she wrote that?

BARBARA: She was older, I think, maybe fifties or sixties.
In the very first paragraph she sees her first lover and he
says something like, "Rather than your face as a young
woman, I prefer it as it is now. Ravaged." And she's older,
looking back.

BOBBIE: A few years ago, I got sick and lost a lot of
patience. Now it's hard for me to pick up serious books
and start reading them without feeling manipulated. For
a long period of time, in literary books a happy ending
would imply that the writer was not serious. Somebody
had to die. I simply couldn't bear the disappointment.
The older I got, the more disaster I accumulated. It finally
just wore me down. I couldn't read a book that ended by
killing off the people I wanted to be happy. It was finally
too much.

BARBARA: Yes, I guess that's one of the reasons our
reading habits shift as we grow older. *One Small Saga*,
however, does not have a disastrous ending. Somewhere
near the end I remember Jesse (you) saying to a friend,
"I like living my life. This is like heaven to me." [...]
I think the only time you felt out of place was with Olaf's
sisters, right?

BOBBIE: My dear, I didn't at all feel out of place. If I wanted to be some place, I usually felt I had the right to be there.

BARBARA: When you got to British Honduras, how was it living there? You had lived in the United States—in Texas and New Mexico—and then you found yourself in this completely different culture.

BOBBIE: We went from Denmark to London for a year. I signed into the Slade, the painting section of London University College. I was there as a special student because we believed that within a year's time, the person who had gone to Africa in Olaf's place would be coming back to London and then we would be going to Africa. When I went to the Slade to sign in, I explained to them that I wouldn't be there as a regular student and they let me give them some money to go there daily. I got to work with models and make drawings and some paintings. I made friends with Lucien Freud. We used to go out and have Turkish coffee. Olaf and I were in West Hampstead, living at that point in a bedsit, one room, with a kind of single burner fixed about ten inches off the floor that you had to feed shillings into it if you wanted to cook something. I'd sit on the floor to cook. There was a sink in the room and the bathroom we shared with others was down the hall.

Olaf loved going to the theater so we got to go to the theater often. We saw *Streetcar Named Desire* with Vivien Leigh and *Mister Roberts*. My life became very rich and it felt more like where I belonged. So there we were.

After we had been in London a year, Olaf's firm decided to close down their Lagos office. He went looking for another job and got one with the Colonial Development

Corporation. They wanted to build a hotel in Belize because Belize was getting none of the tourist trade. Olaf was to be the resident architect. We got on a banana boat to Jamaica, from Jamaica we would be flying to Belize. At that point, I was eight months pregnant with my first daughter. The stewardess on the boat was horrified that a person who was that pregnant would be let on the boat. She kept her eye on me. When we got into warm weather the crew rigged up a swimming pool and a very hefty woman offered me the use of her second bathing suit. The food on the ship was fantastic. In London, we had been severely rationed, and suddenly we were being given menus that read like a fantasy. The week before we left London, Jamaica had played cricket at Lords against England and won. One of the bowlers for the Jamaican team was on our banana boat, returning to Jamaica. When we arrived in Kingston, all the piers were filled with welcomers, playing calypsos and steel drums, and welcoming their hero, Valentine. No one was allowed to leave the ship. It was charming, seeing the Lord Mayor of Kingston in his formal robes and all of this procedure. Of course, some of the passengers were aggravated that they were held up because of this ceremony, but I was delighted. [...] Then, in Belize I found myself in this British colonial situation.

BARBARA: Did you feel uncomfortable in that situation?

BOBBIE: I was living in a book I'd read. I was in the romance. I had a handsome husband, a new baby, a cook and a nursemaid. I met some wonderful women. They were articulate, had been all over the world and they treated me kindly. Belize which was then British Honduras was a third ranking colony, a colony that brought in no income, so that everything that was sustained there was sustained by England and they paid for everything. They even paid the police.

One of the first things Olaf did when we got there was buy a sailboat, an eighteen foot seagull, and that was the first time I'd ever sailed. They had a yacht club, but it was only palmettos pounded into the bottom of the ocean with two platforms, like a first floor, and once a month everyone would congregate there, and we'd have a race. Then there were three clubs and one of them was pretty patently a colonial club with regular dances and dinners. People were very nice to me because I was very young, and my manners weren't all that bad. So it was easy. It was a lot of information. I had in my mind that out in front of me there was this woman who would be elegant and, and it was as if I were en route to that.

BARBARA: Did you get there?

BOBBIE: Oh God, nobody ever gets there.

London, 1949

late 1980s / early 1990s

Photograph used for the original publications of *One Small Saga* and *En Route*.

Growing up in West Texas, **BOBBIE LOUISE HAWKINS** (1930-2018) was raised on the family tales her grandmother told. Having spent her childhood reading, Hawkins believed she would someday live in the world she only read about in books. Her life and work intersected with both that of the Beat Generation and the Black Mountain poets. She wrote more than twenty books of fiction, non-fiction, poetry, and performance monologues.

She performed her work at in New York City (Joseph Papp's Public Theater, Bottom Line, and Folk City), in San Francisco (The Great American Music Hall, and Intersection), as well as reading and performing in Canada, England, Germany, Japan, Holland, and elsewhere. In England she worked with Apples and Snakes and read at the Canterbury Festival and the Poetry Society. A one-hour play, "Talk" (1980), aired on the PBS show "The Listening Ear." She has a record, with Rosalie Sorrels and Terry Garthwaite, *Live At the Great American Music Hall* (Flying Fish), and another, *Jaded Love*, with Lee Christopher and the Al Hermann Quartet (Bijou Press). She was also a visual artist known specifically for her collage work.

In 1978, she was invited by Anne Waldman and Allen Ginsberg to establish a prose concentration in the writing program at Naropa University where she taught for twenty years.

BARBARA HENNING is the author of four novels and seven collections of poetry, including a recent novel, *Just Like That*; a book of poems, *A Day Like Today*; and a collection of object-sonnets, *My Autobiography*. She is the editor of *Looking Up Harryette Mullen* and *The Collected Prose of Bobbie Louise Hawkins*. Born in Detroit, she presently lives in Brooklyn and teaches for Long Island University and writers.com.

LAIRD HUNT is the author of seven novels, with an eighth, *Zorrie*, forthcoming from Bloomsbury USA in early 2021. He is the winner of the Anisfield-Wolf Book Award for Fiction, the Grand Prix de Littérature Américaine, the Bridge Prize, and was a finalist for both the Pen/Faulkner and the Prix Femina Étranger. His reviews and essays have been published in *The New York Times*, *The Washington Post*, and *The Wall Street Journal*, among others. A former United Nations press officer, he lives in Providence where he teaches in Brown University's Literary Arts Program.

ELENI SIKELIANOS is the author of two hybrid memoir/family histories (*The Book of Jon*, City Lights; *You Animal Machine*, Coffee House) and eight books of poetry, most recently *What I Knew* (Nightboat, 2019). Sikelianos is the recipient two National Endowment for the Arts fellowships and the National Poetry Series, among other awards. She was Bobbie Louise Hawkins' student in the late 1980s and early '90s, and her colleague at Naropa beginning in the early 2000s. She currently teaches at Brown University.

The Lost Literature Series at Ugly Duckling Presse is dedicated to neglected works of twentieth century poetry and prose, and resonant works that fall outside these confines.